THE KINGFISHER TREASURY OF

Magical
Stories

D0190348

For Jan Jan,
with much love – F. W.

For Bobo and Chunka – P. A.

.

KINGFISHER
An imprint of Kingfisher Publications Plc
New Penderel House, 283-288 High Holborn
London WC1V 7HZ
www.kingfisherpub.com

First published by Kingfisher 2003
This edition published by Kingfisher 2006
2 4 6 8 10 9 7 5 3 1

A CIP catalogue record for this book is available from the British Library

ISBN-13: 978 0 7534 1341 8
ISBN-10: 0 7534 1341 8

Printed in India
1TR/1105/THOM/(MA)/115IWF

THE KINGFISHER TREASURY OF

Magical Stories

CHOSEN BY FIONA WATERS

ILLUSTRATED BY PETER BAILEY

KINGFISHER

CONTENTS

THE LITTLE WORLD, THE LITTLE SUN AND THE WONDERFUL CHILD

Margaret Mahy

Far far out in the darkness of space, lost among the great galaxies, was one little pinkish sun with a tiny world going round and round it. That world grew roses, strawberries and oranges. It had little oceans and little lands and on one of the lands in the middle of a forest lay a large, lonely green egg. Neither the sun nor the world could remember how that egg had got there.

There was no bird to sit on that egg and keep it safe and warm, but the pink sun shone on it in a friendly way and one day suddenly – BANG – it hatched out.

Out came a child with wings who looked right and left around the world and then looked up at the sun and laughed with pleasure. Neither the sun nor the world had ever heard anyone laugh before.

"There is someone living and laughing on me,"

cried the world in amazement.

"I will make day and night for him," cried the sun.

The wonderful winged child laughed and sang. When he stood up in the forest the trees reached to his waist. He played all over the world, eating strawberries and oranges as he played.

"He's getting bigger and bigger," said the little world. "Perhaps he might like an apple tree and a fountain of lemonade. I think I could manage that."

The child grew and grew, smelling the roses, swimming in the oceans and drinking from the lemonade fountain.

"He's getting so big it's hard to keep him warm all over," said the sun.

"He steps from island to island," said the world proudly. "What a wonderful child I have."

"He's mine too," said the sun. "I kept him warm when he was an egg."

The child grew and grew. He spread out his wings and swept a forest into the sea.

"Alas the day and well-a-way!" sighed the world, sorry to see one of its forests go.

"Well-a-way! Alas the day!" sighed the little sun. "You poor child! Part of you is always on the night side of the world."

The child smiled and grew a little more.

"Dear child, you are getting too big for me," lamented the little world. "I am starting to crumple around the edges. Look! You've squashed my South Pole."

And then for the first time the giant child spoke.

"The time has come to fly," he cried, and he leaped into the air and flew. His bright hair burned like the flare of a rocket, and as he flew he grew and grew. Round and round the little world he flew, then round and round the little sun, smiling in at them.

"Don't go!" cried the little sun. "We'll be lonely without you. Oh dear! I'm going to cry and if I cry I might put myself out."

"I don't want to be empty again," said the little world. "Roses and apples and strawberries are beautiful. Forests and oceans are wonderful, and I am very proud of the lemonade fountain, but I really need a child with wings too."

"I'll take you with me," said the giant child. He took the sun in one hand as if it were a lamp, and the world in the other as if it were an apple. Then he flew off through space.

Comets followed him like playful dogs. Meteors burnt up like candles, lighting his way.

They passed a world with two suns.

"Not as beautiful as you," said the child to the world in his right hand.

They passed a rather conceited sun with ten worlds and a whole lot of moons.

"Not as beautiful as you," said the child to the sun in his left hand.

The dragons and firedrakes who live out in deep space flew around the wonderful child and sang to him.

"We're certainly seeing the universe," the little world and the little sun called to one another.

There were many worlds to be seen, both dark and light, but at last they came to a great red sun – a huge sun – and swinging around it was a thundering, thumping great world with huge oceans and vast forests.

"I might be able to live on that world without

crumbling it," murmured the giant child and he
flew around this world on his great wings. "And it
is quite empty."

"No it isn't!" screamed a million little voices. "We're here! We're here! Lost in the forest."

"Who are you? Where are you?" called the giant child. "I can't see you."

"We are the ladybird people," the voices called back. "You can't see us because we're nothing much on this thumping, thundering great world. Oh, if only we had a ladybird-sized world where we could find one another."

"I have a wonderful little world in my right hand and a beautiful sun in my left hand," called the child. "I'll put them here in this empty bit of space. While I settle them down you pack yourselves some lunches . . . several lunches. Then I'll put one wing tip down on your big world and one wing tip on the little world, and you can run up one wing, across my shoulders and down my other wing. You can live on the little world, and I'll live on the big one and we can be neighbours. The South Pole on the little world is a bit squashed, but there is a lovely lemonade fountain. You'll really enjoy it."

The child put the little sun and the little world in an empty bit of space, and then he stretched out his giant wings so that one wing touched the big world and one wing touched the little world. The ladybird people swarmed up his wings and crossed from one world to the other. It was a long, long journey, several lunches long.

Now the little world had a whole population of ladybird people. They loved the strawberries and the lemonade fountain. Now the big world was lived on by a giant child – a magical child.

Sometimes he would fly out across space to dance around the little pink sun and the little world and sing to them. He wouldn't come too close in case the storm of his wings blew the forests over but they could hear his song quite clearly.

"There he is – our oldest child," they said proudly to one another. "He is doing well."

Nobody ever found out just who had laid the egg on the little world in the first place. But outer space is like that . . . full of mysteries . . . and you never know what is going to happen next when you get out there among the stars.

TAMLANE

A Scottish Fairy Tale
Retold by Winifred Finlay

A long time ago — so long ago that everyone now has forgotten exactly when — the Queen of the Faeries used to hold her court by night at Carterhaugh near Selkirk, where Ettrick Water sweeps round to join Yarrow Water before they both flow into the River Tweed.

Winter can be long and cruel in the high moors and lonely dales of the Borderland, and when the north wind skirled and shrieked through the leafless trees and blew the snow higher than walls and barns and cottages, the maidens of Ettrickdale and Yarrow, sitting in their bowers and sewing their silken seams, would drop their needlework and sigh for the spring when they could meet again on the pleasant plain of Carterhaugh.

Nowhere in all the brave Borderland, they

thought, was there grass as green as the grass of Carterhaugh, nowhere were the wild roses so delicate a pink, the bluebells so pure a colour, the broom such a blaze of gold; how pleasant it was, they thought, to meet there and gather flowers and play at ball and talk and laugh and dance and sing,  remembering always to return to their homes before the sun set – because in the hours of darkness the plain belonged to the Little People.

Of all the maidens who played and talked and laughed and danced and sang on the green grass when the winter was past, the fairest and most courageous was the Lady Janet, whose parents loved her dearly and whose father had given her the land of Carterhaugh for her own.

One bright May morning she was playing with four and twenty other maidens; they were throwing high a coloured ball, laughing as they picked up their long silken dresses to run, barefoot, to catch it, when the Queen of the Faeries suddenly appeared in their midst.

15

"This is the last time you maidens may play here," she said in a cold, thin voice. "I forbid you to set foot again on the grass of Carterhaugh by day or by night, for now it belongs to young Tamlane." And she disappeared as suddenly as she had appeared.

Frightened, the maidens ran for their slippers and hastily pulled them on and braided up their hair, ready to obey the command of the Queen of Faeries – all except the Lady Janet.

"What right has she to say that we cannot play here?" fair Janet cried angrily. "This land is mine. My daddy gave it to me. The Little People are welcome to come here at night, but by day it is mine, and I shall come here whenever I want. And you'll all come and play here with me, won't you?"

But the four and twenty maidens shook their heads, because they were frightened of angering the Faery Queen, and they hurried back to their homes by the banks of the Yarrow and Ettrick Water, leaving fair Janet alone on the green plain, so that in the end she followed them with a sigh.

Yet when she got back to Bowhill, where she

lived, she said nothing to her parents about the Queen of the Faeries.

When she awoke the next morning, she stretched her arms above her head, watched the first ray of the morning sun steal through the window, and wondered what she should do that day.

"I know," she thought. "I shall pick some flowers for my mammy, who loves me more than anything else in all the world. I shall pick her wild roses which are just tinged with pink, and the loveliest roses of all grow on the thorn bush by the well at Carterhaugh, which belongs to me."

Putting on her silken dress, which was as green as the grass on Carterhaugh, and her slippers, which were as red as the berries on the rowan tree, she combed out her long yellow hair and plaited it and wound the plait round her head and fixed it in place with two golden combs on which sparkled emeralds, as green as her dress or the grass of Carterhaugh.

She gathered her long skirts in her hands and ran off to the meadow, to the thorn bush which grew by the well, and she had just picked the first white rosebud, so faintly tinged with pink, when an angry voice behind her cried, "Who are you? And what are you doing here at Carterhaugh?"

When Janet turned round, she saw before her a faery knight on a milk-white steed, which was shod with two shoes of silver and two of gold; the knight himself was dressed from head to foot in white, and on his dark, curling hair he wore a hat with a rose pink plume.

"Who are you? And what are you doing here at

Carterhaugh?" the knight repeated.

"I am the Lady Janet," the maiden answered proudly. "And I am picking wild roses for my mammy because all this land belongs to me. My daddy gave it to me."

"I am Tamlane," the knight cried angrily, looking at Janet with eyes as cold and grey as the waters of Ettrick on a February day. "The Queen of the Faeries gave Carterhaugh to me, and you come here at your peril."

"From sunset to sunrise all this land is yours," fair Janet said. "Is that not enough for you?"

Slowly Tamlane shook his head and his milk-white

steed whinnied and pawed the ground.

"Yesterday I played here with four and twenty maidens," Janet said, "and there was room enough for all of us and room to spare; today there should be room for you and me." And turning to the thorn bush, she continued picking the white rosebuds so faintly tinged with pink.

The anger faded from Tamlane's face and into his grey eyes came a strange, lost look.

"As you have come to gather wild roses for your mammy," he said, "today you may stay. But after this, Carterhaugh is mine and mine alone."

Without saying a word, fair Janet picked the last of the wild roses, and then she turned and stared up into the blue, blue sky, listening to the liquid trilling of the skylark which hovered overhead; and Tamlane turned his head and looked up with his sad grey eyes and sighed. "So long ago is it since last I heard the song of the lark on a May morning, that I had almost forgotten how beautiful it could be," he said, and tugging at the reins of his milk-white steed, he galloped off without another word, and Janet picked up the skirts of her silken dress in her left hand and walked slowly back to her home.

The next morning when she awoke she stretched her arms above her head and watched the first rays of the morning sun steal through the window, wondering what she should do that day.

"I know," she thought. "I shall pick some flowers

for my mammy, who loves me more than anything else in all the world. I shall pick her sprays of green broom afire with golden blossom, and the finest bush with the richest flowers grows not far from the well at Carterhaugh, which belongs to me."

Putting on her silken dress, which was as green as the grass on Carterhaugh, and her slippers, which were as red as the berries on the rowan tree, she combed out her long yellow hair and plaited it, and wound the plait round her head, and fixed it in place with two golden combs on which sparkled emeralds, as green as her dress or the grass of Carterhaugh.

She gathered her long skirts in her hand and ran off to the meadow, to the broom which grew near the well. She had just broken off the first branch, when an angry voice behind her cried, "Who are you? And what are you doing here at Carterhaugh?"

When Janet turned round, she saw before her Tamlane on his milk-white steed, which was shod with two shoes of silver and two of gold; but this time the plume in his hat was gold like the blossom of the broom.

"I am the Lady Janet," the maiden answered quietly, "and I am picking golden broom for my mammy, because all this land belongs to me."

"It belongs to me!" Tamlane cried angrily, and his grey eyes were as cruel as Yarrow Water when the snows melt on the hills and the river thunders down in search of victims among the weary sheep or the travellers who have lost their way.

"Yesterday I picked my mammy a bunch of wild roses and together we listened to the lark as it sang high up in the blue, blue sky," Janet said softly. "There was room enough for the two of us then, Tamlane, so why should there not be room today?" And turning to the bush, she continued picking the green branches with their golden blossom.

The anger faded from Tamlane's face and into his grey eyes there came again a strange, lost look.

"As you have come to gather broom for your mammy," he said, "today you may stay.

But after this, Carterhaugh is mine and mine alone."

Without saying another word, fair Janet picked the last spray of golden broom, and then she sat down on the green grass and looked across the Yarrow to the distant moorlands and listened to the plaintive cry of the curlew; and Tamlane looked down at fair Janet with his sad grey eyes and sighed.

"So long is it since last I heard the song of the curlew on a May morning, that I had almost forgotten how beautiful it could be," he said, and he tugged at the reins of his milk-white steed and galloped off without another word, and Janet gathered the skirts of her silken dress in her right hand and walked slowly back to her home.

When fair Janet awoke the following morning, she made up her mind to gather for her mammy a bunch of wild hyacinths, and because the loveliest and bluest flowers grew by the well of Carterhaugh, she picked up her long green dress in one hand and ran off to the meadow.

When she reached the well, Tamlane was waiting for her on his milk-white steed, and the plume in his hat was blue like the bells of the wild hyacinth. This time, instead of challenging her, he watched in silence as she pulled the long-stemmed bluebells and then, when her bunch was complete, he dismounted

and together they walked down to the banks of the Yarrow and sat there, listening to the melancholy cry of the peewit. And Tamlane looked at fair Janet and sighed. "So long is it since last I heard the cry of the peewit that I had almost forgotten how beautiful it could be," he said.

"Are there no birds in Faeryland," fair Janet asked, "that you sigh when you hear the song of the skylark and the sound of the curlew and the cry of the peewit?"

"The faeries have their own sweet music to dance to and have no need of the song of the birds," Tamlane answered. "But memory dies hard with me, for I am mortal born.

"My father was Randolph, Earl of Murray; my mother the sweetest lady in the land. But the Queen of the Faeries spied me when I was out hunting one day and wanted me to be her courtier. She sent a cold wind from the north that chilled me to the marrow and I fell from my horse and lay in a swoon on the ground.

"The Faery Queen had me carried to yonder green hill, where she tended me with magic herbs and many a strange charm. And now I am Tamlane, her favourite knight, and with each successive day my mortal memory fades like some dimly remembered dream."

"And are you not content to live in Faeryland, where everyone is happy and no one is ever ill?" fair Janet asked.

"Once I might have been content," Tamlane answered, "but now that I have met you, Janet, I wish with all my heart the spell could be lifted so that I might wed you."

"What the Queen of Faeries can do, that I can undo," Janet said, "because I too shall not be content until you are a mortal man and wed me. Tell me what must be done and I will do it."

"The spell is powerful, and to break it you will

need more courage than any other maiden in all the Borderland. You must return to your home and go your way throughout the summer and the autumn, giving no thought to Tamlane, and avoiding by day and night the green plain of Carterhaugh.

"And then, on the last night of October, which is Hallowe'en, if you have courage enough to try to break the spell, fair Janet, then go to Miles Cross and wait there, because the Faery Queen with all her knights and courtiers will ride past on the stroke of midnight, on her way to dance on the green grass of Carterhaugh."

"But how shall I know you among so many valiant knights and brave courtiers?" fair Janet asked.

"Listen to me carefully, Janet," Tamlane said, "because then my fate will be in your hands, and though Faeryland is indeed beautiful, my heart longs to be with you and with my own kind again.

"When you stand by the cross on Hallowe'en, first you will hear the sound of faery pipes and the beating of faery drums, and a standard bearer carrying a red banner will lead past the first company; but do not stir or move a muscle, for I shall not be among them.

"And then a standard bearer carrying a green banner will lead past the second company, but do not stir or move a muscle, for I shall not be among them.

"But when the standard bearer carrying a white banner leads past the third company, then look for me, Janet. The first knight will wear black armour and be mounted on a steed as black as midnight, but he will not be Tamlane. And the armour of the second knight will be as brown as a chestnut to match the colour of his steed, but he will not be Tamlane. But the third knight will be clad in white and will be riding a milk-white steed, and he will be your Tamlane, Janet.

"I shall wear a gold star on my forehead and a glove on my right hand, but my left hand will be bare. As soon as you see me, seize the bridle reins and pull me from my horse, and then, Janet, hold me fast no matter what happens, for the Faery Queen will be bitterly angry and will use every trick she knows to make you let me go, and if once you do, I shall be lost to you for ever."

"I shall do as you say and break the spell that binds you to the Faery Queen," fair Janet promised, and she went back to her home, and never during the summer or the autumn did she return to Carterhaugh.

27

When the last night of October came, Janet wrapped herself in her grass green cloak and set out in the moonlight for Miles Cross. With an anxious heart she waited, and presently she heard the sound of faery pipes and the beating of faery drums and she knew that the procession was on its way past the cross to dance on the green at Carterhaugh.

First came the standard bearer carrying the red banner, but Janet hid behind the cross and let his company pass because Tamlane was not among them.

And then came the standard bearer with the green banner, and again Janet kept herself hidden because Tamlane was not among that company. But when the standard bearer carrying the white banner approached, then Janet knew

the time had come. With fast beating heart she watched as a knight, in black armour, mounted on a steed as black as midnight, rode past, but he was not Tamlane. And she watched as the second knight, in brown armour to match the colour of his steed, rode past, but he was not Tamlane.

But the third knight rode a milk-white steed: his armour was white and he wore a gold star on his forehead and a glove on his right hand, but his left hand was bare. And he was Tamlane.

Summoning all her courage, Janet ran forward; seizing the bridle of the milk-white horse, she pulled Tamlane off its back and held him in her arms. Immediately the faeries cried out in alarm and anger, and the Queen of the Faeries spurred her horse forward.

"So you think you can escape!" she cried furiously, and lifting one finger of her right hand, she changed Tamlane into a green lizard that quivered and wriggled and struggled to be free. But Janet looked into the creature's soft grey eyes, and held it fast and would not let it go.

Darker grew the face of the Faery Queen; now she lifted up her right hand, and immediately Tamlane was changed into a green snake which curved and writhed and struggled to be free. But Janet gazed into its sorrowful eyes, and held it fast and would not let it go.

"So you would match yourself against the Queen of the Faeries!" the Queen cried, lifting her right arm, and now Tamlane was a wild deer, kicking and fighting and struggling to be free. But Janet gazed into its imploring eyes, and held it fast and would not let it go.

And the Queen of the Faeries realized that now, at last, Janet had broken the spell and that there was nothing she could do to keep Tamlane in her service. Slowly she raised her left hand and changed Tamlane into his mortal shape. At once fair Janet threw her green cloak over him and together they stood by the cross and watched as the faery procession, with the Queen in its midst, rode on to Carterhaugh.

The next day, which was Hallo'day, fair Janet and Tamlane plighted their troth, and on Ne'erday, which is the first day of the New Year, the bells of the steeple of Selkirk Church pealed joyously to announce to all the good people who dwelt by Yarrow and Ettrick Water that Tamlane, son of the Earl of Murray, who had once been bewitched by the Queen of the Faeries, had just wed the fair Lady Janet, whose love and whose courage had broken the spell and set him free.

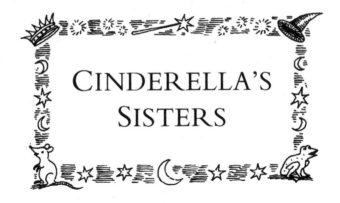

CINDERELLA'S SISTERS

Margaret Baker

Do you remember the tale of Cinderella, and all about the fairy godmother and the pumpkin coach and the glass slipper and the two ugly sisters? Of course you remember it; but have you ever wondered what happened to the ugly sisters after the Prince had handed Cinderella into his carriage and driven away to be married? Listen, and I will tell you the tale.

When they were left alone the ugly sisters threw themselves into their chairs and wept – wept such hot, jealous tears that their eyes smarted as though someone had thrown pepper in them. And when they could weep no more for envy, they began to weep from temper – tears as sour as though they had been mixed with vinegar. And when they could weep no more for any reason at all, they began to quarrel, and to sob and sigh and wish they were dead.

"I must have my smelling-salts at once," said one, and rang the bell.

"I feel quite faint; I must have some tea immediately," said the other, and rang the bell in her turn.

But of course no one came.

They stormed and they whimpered, but that did no good at all, and at last they began to realize the disagreeable fact that they would have to wait on themselves.

They went downstairs to the kitchen; but one bruised her hand at the pump as she tried to fill the kettle, and the other burned her fingers as she tried to mend the fire, and down they sat among the cinders, quarrelling and weeping more than ever.

Who should come and find them there but the fairy godmother.

"Farthings and fiddle-sticks!" cried she. "What is the meaning of this?"

"*You* should know that better than anyone else!" said the first sister sulkily. "What do you mean by taking Cinderella away?"

"Fancy sending that little cinder-wench to the ball and leaving us behind!" cried the second. "A fine muddle you have made of things!"

"And using *our* pumpkin to make her a coach!" added the first.

"Go away at once!" they cried together.

"I shall go when I am ready," said the fairy godmother, and drew herself up as tall as she could, which was not very tall, in spite of her high-heeled shoes. "This seems a comfortable and convenient house, and I need a rest and change; I think I shall stay here for a long visit."

"We couldn't allow it for a minute!" cried the sisters. "What an idea!"

The fairy godmother lifted her stick. "Take care!" she warned them. "If I can turn pumpkins into coaches, and lizards into footmen, you may be sure I know how to turn people into toads and caterpillars if I have the fancy."

Toads and caterpillars! The ugly sisters screamed at the very idea!

"I said I could do it *if* I had the fancy," said the fairy godmother. "As long as you make me comfortable and behave politely I shall not take the trouble to turn you into anything at all. Come, come, bestir yourselves! There is my tea to get ready and the spare bed to air!"

The ugly sisters tossed their heads and began to say she had better get the tea ready herself if she wanted any; but they remembered about the toads and caterpillars just in time and went sulkily to do as they were told.

The fairy godmother made herself very much at home; she ordered the sisters about from morning to night, and a very hard mistress they found her. She never seemed to tire of scolding and fault-finding, and she made them work as hard and fare as scantily as ever Cinderella had done. And at night there was nowhere for them to sit but among the ashes on the kitchen hearth.

It went on for a year and a day, and then there was to be a ball at the palace grander than any that had gone before.

When evening came the sisters sat sadly in the chimney corner and listened to the coaches rattling by.

"We might have been going to the ball too, if we had not treated Cinderella so badly!" sighed the first. "How happy we might have been together!"

"We deserve to be punished for our temper and selfishness!" sighed the second.

At that very moment they heard the tap-tap of the fairy godmother's high-heeled shoes on the kitchen stairs.

"Heyday!" cried she. "Hasten! Hasten! You will be late for the ball!"

"For the ball!" cried the first sister. "But how are we to go?"

"For the ball!" cried the second. "But we have nothing to wear!"

"Leave that to me!" said the fairy godmother, and in the twinkling of an eye the sisters found themselves dressed from head to heel in silks and satins as beautiful as though they were made of butterfly wings sewn with dewdrops, and from the street came the sound of a carriage drawing up at the door with a jingle of bells and a cracking of whips.

The fairy godmother nodded her head as she saw their surprise. "You think that is wonderful magic," said she, "but I have done even more wonderful things for you without any magic at all. Have you looked in the mirror?"

Strange as it may seem, the sisters had not thought of trying to admire themselves for many a long day. Now when they ran to the mirror they could hardly believe their eyes, for all the lines and wrinkles had disappeared with the ugly thoughts and idle ways that had made them, and they were almost as beautiful as Cinderella herself.

So the sisters went to the ball with the fairy godmother, and the Princess Cinderella ran all the way down the room to welcome them, and everyone was as merry as merry could be.

And did the sisters marry princes and live happily ever after? Of course they did, for in fairy tales people always get what they deserve.

UNDER THE MOON

Vivian French

Once upon a time there was a little old woman and a little old man who lived together in a little old house. They would have been very happy but for one thing: the little old woman just could not sit still. Never ever did she sit down and share a cup of cocoa with the little old man. Dust dust dust, polish polish polish, shine shine shine – all day long she was busy.

The little old man began to sigh, and to grow lonely. While their ten tall children were growing up in their neat little house he didn't have time to notice how the little old woman never stopped working. Now, however, he liked to sit by the fire and dream, and he thought it would be a friendly thing if the little old woman sat beside him.

"You could knit a little knitting," said the little old man, "or sew a little seam?"

But the little old woman said, "No, no, no! I must dust and sweep and clean."

The little old man sighed a long sad sigh and went and put the kettle on. He sat down beside the fire with Nibbler the dog and Plum the cat, and Nibbler curled up at his feet and Plum curled up on his lap, but still the little old man felt lonely.

The little old woman went on sweeping the yard with her broom, even though the stars were beginning to twinkle in the sky.

One day there was a knocking on the door.

"Who's there?" asked the little old woman, running to open the door with her duster in one hand and her mop in the other.

"It's me," said young Sally from the cottage down the road. "My mum says you'm the bestest cleaner in all the village, and we've just got two new babies as like as two peas, and all the children running here and there with smuts on their noses and dirt on their toeses, and our mum was a-wondering . . . ?"

The little old woman didn't wait another moment. She picked up her broom as she ran through the door, and she fairly flew down the road to Sally's cottage. All day she polished and swept and scrubbed, and by the time the stars were twinkling the cottage down the road was as shiny as a new pin; as fresh as a daisy; as polished as a one minute chestnut fallen from the tree.

"Well, well, well," said the little old man as she hurried through the door. "There's a good day's work you've done. Would you like a little cocoa?"

The little old woman actually sat down.

"Thank you kindly, my dear," she said. "Just a sip or two — and then I must polish our own little house." And she sat quietly beside the little old man for five minutes.

"This is fine and dandy," said the little old man, smiling. Nibbler laid his head on the little old woman's feet, and Plum purred happily.

"Just as it should be of a gentle summer evening," said the little old man.

"No, no, no!" said the little old woman. She

drank the last drop of cocoa and jumped to her feet. "It was very nice, but I must hurry hurry hurry." And she seized the duster and hurried off to the dresser full of china to polish and shine. The little old man sighed, but it was a medium-sized sigh.

"Five minutes is five minutes more than nothing," he said. Nibbler nodded his head.

The next day brought another knocking on the door.

"Who's there?" said the little old woman, running to the door with her dustpan in one hand and a broom in the other.

"It is I," said the parson from the church across the hill. "I have heard that you are the most wonderful cleaner in the county, and my church is full of mice and moths and mildew."

The little old woman jumped to her feet. She picked up her soap and a bucket as she ran through the door, and she hurried and scurried to the church across the hill. She swept and she dusted and she rubbed, and by the end of the day the church was glowing as if a hundred candles had been lit inside.

"Well, well, well," said the little old man as she walked through the door. "There's another good day's work done. Could you fancy a cup of cocoa?"

"Thank you kindly," said the little old woman, and she sat down on the bench by the fire with a flop.

"Just a small cup, and then I must scrub our own back yard." But she sat quietly with the little old man and with Nibbler the dog and Plum the cat for ten long minutes. Then up she hopped and away she went with the broom in the yard.

The little old man sighed a very little sigh.

"What do you think, Nibbler? Isn't ten minutes ten whole minutes more than nothing?"

Nibbler nodded, and Plum purred.

The next day no one came to the house. The little old woman cleaned and rubbed and scrubbed her little house inside and out, and when the stars began to twinkle in the bluebell sky she was still swishing her soapsuds in the tub. Then there came a knock at the door – such a timid, quiet little knock you could hardly hear it. The little old woman hurried to see who it was, her hands wet and dripping.

"Who's there?" she asked.

Standing on the doorstep was a strange grey shadow of a man. His hair was long and silver, and his clothes were all a-tremble about him.

"I hear," he whispered in a voice as soft as a bird's breath, "that you are the very best cleaner in all the ups and downs of the Earth?"

The little old woman nodded briskly. She shook the water from her hands, and the drops flew through the air.

"How can I help you? she asked.

"It's the cobwebs," said the silvery grey person. "I don't know what to do about them."

The little old woman ran back into the house and picked up her broom and a basket of dusters.

"Just tell me where they are," she said fiercely. "I've never met a cobweb yet that didn't whisk away when I got busy."

44

The silvery grey person waved his arms in the air, and silver dust scattered about him.

"Up there," he whispered, "seventeen times as high as the moon."

The little old woman looked up into the night sky. Sure enough, there, high above the moon, were long trails of cobweb lying across the sky. She hurried inside, and shook the little old man from his doze in front of the rosy crackling fire.

"Come along, my dear," she said, "I need your help."

Nibbler and Plum ran out with the little old man, but when Nibbler saw the stranger he began to whine. He lowered his head, and crawled back into the house with his tail tucked under him. Plum was not afraid. She greeted the grey person as an old friend, purring and rubbing in and out of his legs.

"Whatever is it?" asked the little old man. "We need your help," said the little old woman. She shook the dusters out of the basket, and settled herself and her broom inside.

"Now, my dear, toss me up, just as high as ever you can."

The little old man picked up the basket. He shut his eyes and counted to three. Then, with a heave and a pitch and a toss, he threw the little old woman up and up and up into the air. Up she flew, higher and higher, until the little old man could only see her as a tiny speck against the light of the moon.

The silvery grey stranger bowed a long and quivery bow.

"I do thank you," he said in his soft thread of a voice, and he shook himself all over. Silvery sparkles flew in the air and settled on the little old man and on the ground around him; it made the old man sneeze – once, twice, three times.

When he had stopped sneezing the stranger was gone – flown back to his home in the moon. Looking up, the old man could see his pale face smiling down.

The little old woman came back with the sunlight in the early morning. She slept a little in her rocking chair, and then bustled about the house. It seemed to the little old man that she was not as quick as usual.

When evening came the little old man put on the kettle, and sat down in front of the fire. Nibbler and Plum sat down with him, and so did the little old woman.

"That's a fine night's work," said the little old man, looking up into the clear and starlit sky. "Not a trace of a cobweb can I see."

The little old woman sniffed. "Indeed, I should hope not, my dear," she said. "When has a cobweb ever been too much for me and my broom? I shall be up again next full moon, just to make sure."

"Would you like a little cup of cocoa?" the little old man asked.

"Indeed I would, my dear," said the little old woman. "And, if it's all the same to you, I'll just sit quietly here this evening. It's tiring work, sweeping all those cobwebs away."

The little old man and the little old woman sat happily together. Nibbler slept curled up at their feet, and Plum settled himself on the little old woman's lap.

It was the same the next night and every night until the full moon rose, and then once more the little old woman seated herself in her basket and the little old man tossed her up into the sky.

"Wheeeee!" she called, as she flew up and up and up. "Can you see me, my dear?"

"I can see you," the little old man said, smiling.

"Will you come with me the next time the moon is full?" asked the little old woman.

"No, not I," said the little old man, and he went into the house as the little old woman flew up and away out of sight.

I'll sit by myself tonight, he thought as he put wood on the fire and the kettle on to boil, but she'll be here tomorrow and every night before the next full moon.

Up in the sky the little old woman was sweeping away the cobwebs. Down below the little old man was rocking in his chair, while the kettle bubbled happily on the hearth. The man in the moon smiled at them both, and the silver moon-sparkles glistened and shone in the little old man's hair. Nibbler and Plum slept peacefully, and there was not so much as the smallest of sighs in the little old house under the moon.

THE MAGIC GIFTS

A Cajun Folk Tale
Retold by Fiona Waters

Young Leo lived with his Papa in a ramshackle old cabin. Papa was old and tired – life and Lady Luck had not been kind to him – and Leo worried every daylight hour about taking care of the old man. There came a day when he decided he needed to try his chances with Lady Luck. Leo resolved to go out into the world and earn a living so his old Papa could rest on the porch in sunny comfort.

"I guess it's my turn to look after you, Papa," Leo said, as he packed a few things in a little sack. "You stay here and do some fishin', and I'll come back just as soon as I can, see if I don't."

And off he set, whistling between his teeth. He walked many miles and some more, but nowhere could he find work. Times were hard and no one was going to give a man's job to a boy, however cheerful he might be. Leo became downhearted.

"This ain't going so good," he said to himself, and he slumped down in the dirt by the side of the road and closed his eyes in despair. But as he sat there feeling mighty sorry for himself, he remembered his poor old Papa's face.

"Life ain't been too generous to you, Papa, but never once did I see you give up. Here I am sittin' like an ol' wet rooster, givin' myself grief. Get up, Leo, this here minute and move on down the road. Act like a man!" And after chiding himself, Leo scrambled to his feet, hefted his sack onto his shoulder and set off down the road once more.

After a while, along he came to a rundown farm. The fences needed repair and the farmhouse roof didn't look too safe, but Leo strode into the yard and knocked on the porch door. The farmer appeared and he looked a lot like Leo's own Papa.

"Do you need a hand, Monsieur?" Leo asked, respectful-like.

But even before the farmer could reply, Leo spoke again. "I tell you what, Monsieur. I'm gonna work for you for a whole year. At the end of the year, if you don't like what I done, then you don't pay me. But if I earned my pay, you give it to me then. Ain't got nothin' to lose."

The farmer thought a while, then nodded and shook Leo by the hand. "Well, as you can see, mon petit, I sure do need some help here."

So Leo got busy and worked like a demon. He was the best worker the farmer had ever hired.

The year soon sped by and Leo went to collect his wages.

"If I earned my pay, then I'll thank you for it and be on my way," he said.

"You more than earned it, but, truth is, I don't want you to go, mon petit. How do you reckon on stayin' another year and I'll pay you double then?"

This time it was Leo who figured he had nothing to lose. He had a roof over his head, he had work and he liked the farmer. And double money seemed like a good deal, so they shook hands and Leo went back to work. Now all this time Leo was getting to be an even better worker. He was growing taller and stronger, and he was learning all kinds of new skills.

Another year passed and Leo went to the farmer once more.

"If I earned my pay, then I'll thank you for it and be on my way," he said.

"You more than earned it, but I still don't want you to go, mon petit. You reckon on stayin' another year and I'll pay you triple then?"

Seemed like both the farmer and Leo had a good deal going here. And so Leo stayed for a third year. And the old farmer taught him how to drive a hard bargain at the corn store and how to trade their sweet potatoes and beans for other goods they needed on the farm. And all the while Leo grew taller and stronger.

At the end of the third year, the farmer said to Leo, "I sure am glad you came here to help me, mon petit, but you ain't mon petit any more. You're a grown man, so it's time I paid you and set you on your way."

Leo was happy. He knew he'd done a good job for the farmer, and now it was time to move on. But the farmer had one more lesson for him. He didn't pay Leo in money after all. Instead, he gave him three gifts that might make his fortune or not, depending all on how Leo used them.

First off there was a lasso, but this was no ordinary lasso for it could coil around any object, however small or far away. The second gift was a magical fiddle. Whenever it was played, all those who heard its bewitching music just had to get up and dance, and dance until the tune stopped. The third and final gift was a hat to make the wearer

invisible. Leo was delighted with these gifts. A smart man could make them work very well indeed.

Leo said "merci beaucoup" to the farmer, shouldered his little sack with his three gifts safely inside and set off down the track to see what Lady Luck might offer him. He walked for several days, but nothing fell into his lap, so he decided to put the hat on and see what might happen then.

As he sauntered down the road, he came across a rich-looking gentleman trying to catch a fine red bird fluttering in the cypress trees. But he just couldn't reach high enough into the branches. Leo crept up, all invisible as you will recall, and heard the man say, "Well, I'll be jiggered, missed again! I have got to catch me that bird – it's worth a fortune."

And Leo knew Lady Luck was here and smiling on him at last. He walked over to the gentleman and quickly pulled off the hat. The gentleman nearly jumped out of his skin when Leo suddenly appeared.

"I see you need a man with a sharp eye. I can catch that bird for you, but it will cost you a thousand dollars," Leo said with a slow smile.

Well, the gentleman was keen. "You get that bird for me and I'll pay you," he promised.

Leo swung the magic lasso around and around,

then let it fly. Sure enough, down tumbled the red bird into a thicket of blackberry bushes.

"There you are, monsieur," said Leo. "That will be a thousand dollars, if you please."

But the gentleman was not for paying. He meant to pick up the red bird and run off without paying Leo so much as one thin dime. Shouldering his way through the thicket, he grabbed the bird and said sneeringly to Leo, "I ain't paying nobody for this bird. That was a lucky throw. I don't pay nothing for luck!"

Leo was mad as could be. He reached into his sack, pulled out the magic fiddle and began to play. The rich gentleman found himself compelled to dance even though he was caught fast in the thicket. Before long his clothes were all torn and he was covered in scratches. And still his feet were dancing and dancing.

"Stop, stop!" he hollered. "I'll pay! I'll pay you the thousand dollars!" And he did too, as soon as Leo stopped playing, but he was as mad as an alligator with a toothache. So he went straight to the sheriff and ordered him to arrest the innocent Leo as a con man and a thief.

"You're just a good fer nothin' rascal," said the sheriff, who was all too ready to believe the rich gentleman over a poor, raggedy boy with a tricksy fiddle and a magic hat. So the sheriff handcuffed Leo, marched him to the courtroom and told the judge the whole story, by his way of it, of course.

Now the judge was not going to believe a poor, raggedy boy any more than the sheriff. "We don't like cheats around here, so I tell you what you're going to do. You're going to give this fine gentleman back his thousand dollars and then you're going pay a thousand dollar fine for being too smart by half. And if you don't have the money, why then I'll throw you in jail, and I'll have that tricksy fiddle and the funny hat and that snaky rope too while I'm at it."

Well, Leo was just jumping with rage at the injustice of this, so before anyone could lay a hand on him, he pulled out the fiddle and began to play. Soon the entire courtroom, including the red bird, was jumping. Everyone was dancing and whirling around until they were all breathless.

"Stop, stop! Stop this infernal music," hollered the judge.

"Not until y'all pay me what I reckon you owe me," said Leo. "One thousand dollars for catchin' the bird, one thousand dollars for false arrest and one thousand dollars for tryin' to besmirch my good name." And still he kept playing the magic fiddle.

The judge was mad, the sheriff was mad, the rich gentleman was mad; the rest of the courtroom were just plumb exhausted. Soon feet were blistered and aching, knees were creaking and red faces were puffing and blowing fit to bust. But they couldn't stop dancing.

"All right, all right," cried the judge, the sheriff and the rich gentleman in desperation. "We'll pay up."

But Leo wasn't going to get caught twice. Not until the money was placed into his sack did Leo stop playing the magic fiddle. Everyone collapsed to the floor, and, quick as a flash, Leo put away the fiddle, put on the hat and disappeared as if he had never been there at all. But the judge and the sheriff and the rich gentleman were never to forget the lesson Leo had taught them.

After many days walking, Leo arrived home, and there was his old Papa, hat over his face, asleep on the porch. Leo crept up and dropped the bag of money into his Papa's lap. Never was an awakening more joyful.

"Mon petit, you ain't so petit any more. You're a man, and a man who has met Lady Luck if I guess right by the weight of this bag!" From then on,

Leo and his old Papa went fishing most days, and they were content for many years. Leo never used the magic gifts again — he had no cause to — but he kept them locked away in his trunk until he was the old man. Then, one day, he told *his* son all about the time he left home to find Lady Luck.

DRAGON TROUBLE

Penelope Lively

There were dragons in Cornwall, once. Hundreds of years ago. Or maybe thousands. It could be that there still are, from time to time – just the odd one, here and there. Anyway, this is what happened to a boy of nine called Peter, last summer.

He was spending the holidays with his grandfather, in a small town somewhere around the middle of Cornwall. It was an ordinary little grey stone town with houses and shops and a market square – not the sort of place where you'd expect to find unusual things happening.

Peter's grandfather, though, was rather less ordinary. He lived by himself in a splendidly untidy cottage with a canary in a cage and two rabbits in a hutch in the garden.

When Peter went to stay with him they did

whatever they both felt like and had chips for every meal. Sometimes they stayed in bed till lunch-time and other days they played card games all day and once they decided to make a five foot model aeroplane and sat up all night doing it. I have to tell you that it all came unstuck the next day, but they both felt it had been worth it.

"Don't forget to buy Grandpa a card for his birthday," Peter's mother had said. The day before the birthday, though, Peter decided that just a card would not do for such an excellent grandfather. He went off by himself into the town to look for a present: a rather special present, it would have to be.

Tobacco? No, that was too dull. Chocolates? A corkscrew with a handle in the shape of an anchor? An ashtray with a map of Cornwall on it? Nothing he saw seemed right at all. He wandered into the town square. It was market day and there were fruit and vegetable stalls and shirt and jeans stalls and stalls selling dog food and bird seed, and a great many people. There was also a junk stall at which Peter stopped. This was more promising. He thought about buying a ship in a green glass bottle, but it was much more than he could afford. An old wind-up gramophone would have been just the thing, but that was expensive too.

Then he caught sight of one of those glass domes on a stand that usually have a couple of stuffed birds on a branch under them. This one, though, had a twiggy nest instead, and inside the nest were two large reddish speckled eggs.

As soon as Peter saw it he knew that this would be the perfect present. It might not be what Grandpa had always wanted, but he would want it as soon as he saw it. And it was not too expensive; the glass was cracked and there were several chips out of the stand, so that it had been reduced to two pounds.

Peter bought it.

He was absolutely right: Grandpa was delighted. "Now that's what I call a present," he said. "Original. Not your run-of-the-mill box of handkerchiefs or packet of pipe-cleaners. Just the thing for my mantelpiece."

So the glass dome was put in the centre of the mantelpiece, and that evening, since it was rather chilly, Grandpa lit a fire and he and Peter sat in front of it and ate fish and chips off their knees and admired Peter's present. "Victorian, it'll be," said Grandpa. "A hundred years old or so, I'd reckon."

It was Peter who came down first in the morning. He drew the curtains and had a look at the weather (raining) and then glanced across the room at the glass dome.

Underneath it, something was moving. He stood stock still and stared. Impossible! He moved closer.

The eggs had gone. In their place were two small lizard-like creatures scrabbling frantically at the glass. For a few moments Peter gazed in amazement. Then he rushed upstairs to fetch Grandpa.

Together they inspected the creatures more carefully. They were about five inches long. They had greenish scales blotched with red, legs with tiny claws, long tails with ends barbed like an arrow, and very small . . .

"Wings!" said Grandpa, putting on his glasses. "Would you believe it! Wings – no two ways about it!"

The creatures continued to scrabble at the glass. "What they look like," said Peter, hardly daring to say it, "is dragons."

Grandpa nodded. "You've put your finger on it. What we've got here, to my mind, is a pair of young dragons. Extraordinary! It'll be the heat of the fire that did it. Those eggs must have been laid away in some cold attic all these years. Bring them into the warm and they hatch. It's a wonderful thing, Nature."

Clearly, they could not leave the dragons where they were. Apart from anything else, there would not be enough air for them under the glass. Grandpa found an old cardboard box which they lined with newspaper. Very carefully they lifted the glass dome from its base and tipped the creatures into it.

"Question is," said Grandpa, "what do we feed them on?"

This turned out to be a problem. They tried breadcrumbs, bird food, Kit-E-Kat, banana and lettuce, all of which the dragons ignored. They retreated to the end of the box and sat there forlornly. It wasn't until Grandpa and Peter had their lunch, which was fish fingers and chips,

that they perked up. They began to sniff and scratch at the sides of the box. Peter chopped up a piece of fish finger and offered it to the dragons. They fell on it happily.

The dragons flourished. After a week or so they were getting too big for the box. Grandpa repaired an old rabbit hutch and they moved them out into the garden and put them in that. They ate a packet of fish fingers every day, with a tin of salmon as an occasional treat. Nothing else would they touch, except prawns, which they ate whole, whiskers and all.

Peter and Grandpa were extremely proud of them. "You can keep your budgies and your cats and your dogs," said Grandpa. "I like an unusual pet. And these beat everything, eh?"

The dragons, admittedly, were not especially cosy pets. They did not care for being stroked and were inclined to hiss when disturbed. But they were very handsome. Their scales were now a rich grass-green decorated with reddish-brown spots. They had fine crests along their necks and their tails swished and curled. Their wings were transparent and large enough now to flap. They would sit in their hutch preening and flapping and nibbling at fish fingers.

Given all this, I suppose what came next was inevitable. Grandpa decided to exhibit the dragons at the town's annual Pet Show.

They attracted immediate attention. And caused instant trouble. "What are they, for heaven's sake?" exclaimed the lady in charge of arranging entries.

"Well," said Grandpa, "you've got a point there. I can see they don't fit in with Dogs or Cats or Cage-birds. Reptiles, maybe?"

Eventually, after a great deal of talk among the judges, the dragons were entered in the Miscellaneous Class, along with some tortoises, a tank of newts, two parrots and a grass-snake.

They had a great success. People crowded round their hutch peering through the wire-netting at them and exclaiming. The dragons appeared to enjoy the attention; they strutted up and down and played together. They were now almost the size of rabbits.

The trouble started when it came to the judging. Two of the three judges wanted to give them First Prize but the third objected strongly on the grounds that nobody knew what to call them. Finally a vote was taken. The dragons were given a red rosette, which Grandpa pinned proudly to the hutch.

The awkward judge, a stout woman whose poodle had failed to win a prize in the Dog Class, remarked loudly that the things looked to her like something that ought to be in a museum and she wouldn't be surprised if they carried nasty diseases. She tapped the hutch with her umbrella and then

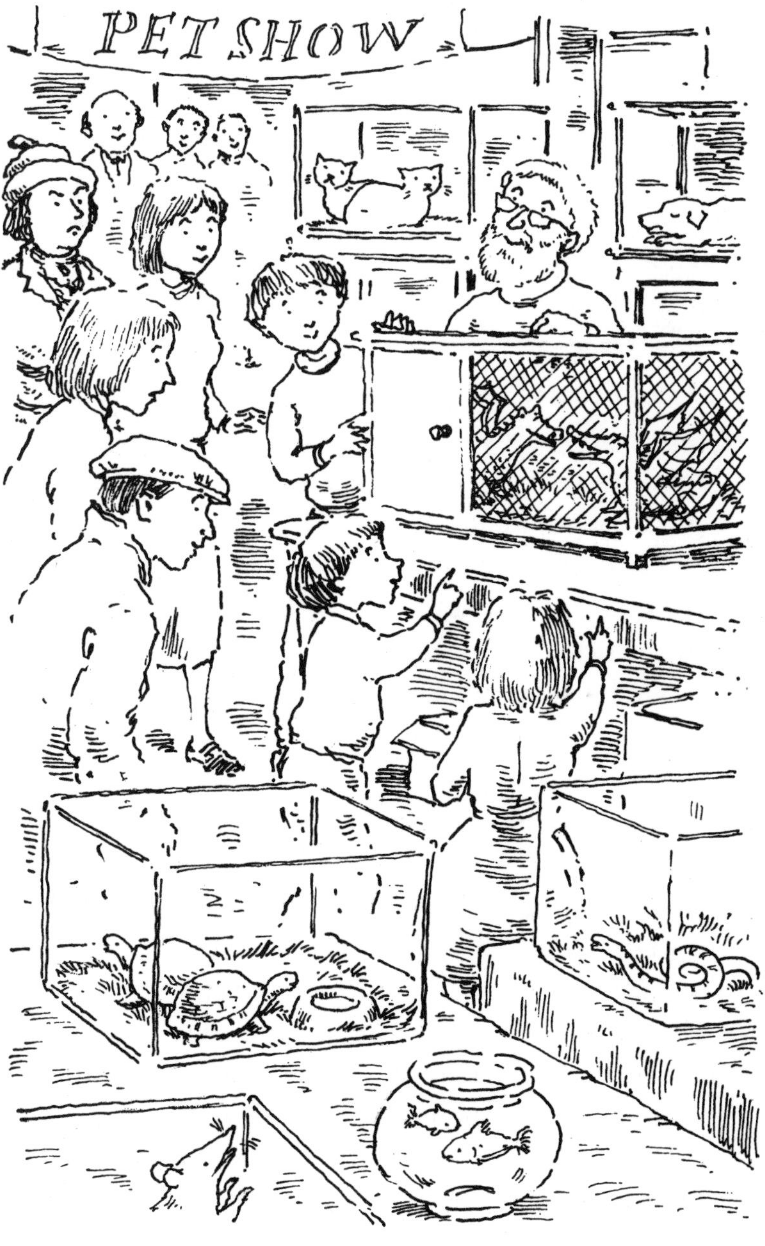
PET SHOW

sprang backwards with a shriek. There was a sizzling sound and a smell of scorching.

The dragons had learned to spit flames. Very small flames, mind you, but flames all the same. Grandpa and Peter took them home hurriedly, before people could ask any more questions or make any more comments than they already were. On the way Grandpa bought a fire extinguisher.

"Just in case. They were provoked, mind. I reckon they'll settle down again once we get them back." He spoke severely to the dragons, who looked now as though butter wouldn't melt in their mouths.

There was a short piece about them in the paper, headed LOCAL PENSIONER'S MYSTERY PETS. Grandpa had mixed feelings about this; he thought the photograph of himself unflattering and he was worried that it would arouse too much curiosity. "There's no limit to how nosy people can be, you take my word for it. Jealous, too. That's what was up with that woman. Plain jealous. Her with her poodle done up like a lamb chop. Next thing, we'll have everyone wanting what we've got. And I'm not breeding them. I've had enough trouble that way with rabbits."

He was right to be worried, as it turned out. Three days later there was a knock at the door and on the step stood a man in uniform who said he was the Pest Control Officer and he had reason to believe that there were some unusual animals in the house. Grandpa and Peter stared at him in alarm.

"Lizards of some sort, is it?" continued the Pest Control Officer. "The name's George, by the way." He held out a printed card to Grandpa. "Mr George. Won't take a minute, but it's my job to check up. All right if I come in?"

They let him in and took him through to the garden. There was nothing else, really, they could do. Mr George squatted down in front of the hutch and studied the dragons. There was a silence.

"Ah," said Mr George. "Yes. I see. A pair of . . . um . . . A pair of those things."

There was a glint, now, in Grandpa's eye. "What," he said, "counts as pests?"

Mr George stood up. "Rats. Mice. Cockroaches. Black beetles. Wasps."

"And are what we've got in that hutch any of those?" continued Grandpa.

"Strictly speaking," said Mr George, "no."

"Then," said Grandpa triumphantly, "what's wrong with us keeping them?"

71

Mr George considered. "Strictly speaking," he said again, "nothing." He cast a doubtful look down at the dragons. "But they're a bit out of the way, you must admit. What . . . um . . . what exactly would you call them now?"

"Dragons," said Peter, before he could help himself.

Mr George laughed. He patted Peter on the head. "Got quite an imagination, your grandson, hasn't he?" he said to Grandpa. "Well, we'll leave it at that for now. But I'll have to make a report on it. And mind you keep them under control – they look to me as though they could give you a nasty nip."

As soon as he had gone Peter and Grandpa heaved signs of relief. It had been a dangerous moment, they agreed. "Someone's been tittle-tattling," said Grandpa darkly. "Her with the poodle, I daresay. Or one of the nosy-parkers in this street. Best thing we can do is lie low. Else . . ."

"Else we mightn't be able to keep them?" said Peter anxiously.

Grandpa nodded.

But there was worse to come. A couple of days later Peter went out in the evening to feed the dragons and found to his horror that the hutch was empty. Part of the wire-netting front had been ripped away, evidently by strong little dragon claws. He and Grandpa searched the garden; there was no sign of them. They remembered with alarm that

lately the dragons had been flapping their wings more and more, like fledglings about to take off. Had they flown right away? Grandpa shook his head sadly. "I don't know as how they'd fend for themselves in that case. How're they going to get across to folk that what they fancy is fish fingers and nothing else?"

"Or tinned salmon," added Peter.

They searched the house, just in case, and then came outside again. And then, both at once, they noticed a curious noise coming from the next door garden. A sound of splashing.

"What's Mrs Hammond up to?" said Grandpa, frowning. Mrs Hammond was the next door neighbour.

"But she's away!" Peter exclaimed. "Don't you remember – she asked us to water her tomatoes for her."

They dashed to the fence and looked over. In the middle of Mrs Hammond's garden was her most treasured possession, a large pond covered with water-lilies and bullrushes amid which swam a couple of dozen fat goldfish.

And there at the edge of the pond was one of the dragons, contentedly munching a goldfish that it held in its front claws.

Even as they watched, the second one rose from a clump of rushes, whooshed up into the air with an untidy flapping of wings and plunged straight down into the pond. A few seconds later it rose to the surface, scrambled out, shook itself like a dog and settled down to eat the goldfish that it, too, was now clutching.

"She's going to be *furious*!" cried Peter.

Grandpa was already rushing into the house. He came out with a piece of green nylon garden netting and a bucket. "Quick! Over that fence!"

Peter scrambled over and set about the difficult business of catching the dragons. Grandpa watched anxiously from the other side and shouted words of advice. The dragons scuttled round the pond hissing angrily and sometimes spitting a few feeble flames. From time to time they took off and flapped a few yards across Mrs Hammond's lawn before flopping to the ground. Evidently they weren't yet very good at flying. At last Peter managed to net them both and get them into the bucket, which he passed over the fence to Grandpa. There were only three goldfish left in the pond.

They put the dragons back in the hutch, where they huddled into the corner still hissing quietly. Peter and Grandpa hurried off to the pet shop in the High Street and they bought the entire stock of goldfish.

"Think she'll notice the difference?" asked Peter when he had emptied them into Mrs Hammond's pond.

Grandpa shook his head. "I doubt if a person gets what you might call close to a fish."

That evening they took a long hard look at the situation. Things could not go on like this.

"You know something?" said Grandpa. "I think I know what it is we've got out there. What we've got is a pair of sea-dragons. Fish-eaters, see? I should have cottoned on to it before."

"Do you think they're full-size yet?" asked Peter.

Grandpa shrugged. "Maybe, maybe not. But one thing I'm clear about; they're getting out of hand. They're not the sort of thing you can keep in your back garden for ever."

The more they thought about it the more it seemed to them that there were only two things they could do. They could give the dragons to a zoo. Or they could let them go.

"They'd hate it in a zoo," said Peter. "Being stared at all the time. And fed peanuts. But where could we let them go?"

"Where they ought to be," said Grandpa. "Their natural habitat. The sea."

And so the great idea was born. It took a lot of planning. They would have to take the dragons to the coast on the bus, since Grandpa did not have a car. Then they would have to find a beach with rocky cliffs from which to launch the dragons.

They borrowed a cat basket from a neighbour (Grandpa spun a story about having to take his rabbits to the vet), got the dragons into it, with some difficulty, and set off. The bus journey was tricky; the dragons scrabbled around in the basket throughout so that Grandpa and Peter had to talk loudly to drown the noise. But at last they reached the coast and set off for a beach where Grandpa knew there were cliffs dropping down into the sea.

There were a good number of people on the beach at the foot of the cliffs. Grandpa and Peter stood at the top of the path that led down there and watched for a few minutes.

"Be all right so long as we can get them off good and quick," said Grandpa. "Straight out to sea and no nonsense."

They opened the cat basket. Peter pushed it nearer to the edge of the cliff. The dragons stuck their heads out and flapped their wings. They climbed onto the edge of the basket and flapped more busily.

"That's it," said Peter. "Shoo! Go on – fly!"

And the dragons took off. They soared upwards and then . . . oh, horrors! . . . they began to sink slowly towards the beach. They spun and flapped and fluttered down at last upon the sand. Peter and Grandpa gave one look, and set off at once helter-skelter down the steep path to the beach.

They got to the spot at which the dragons had landed and began to search for them. People were sitting around having picnics or sunbathing or reading newspapers. There was no sign of the dragons. Suddenly Peter caught sight of one of them. It was sitting beside someone's picnic basket contentedly munching a fish paste sandwich. And the other one was stretched out on the ramparts of some children's sandcastle, sunning itself.

Peter rushed forward to grab them at the same moment as the owner of the fish paste sandwich turned round and gave a cry of alarm. "Excuse me!" Peter panted. "My dog . . ." He snatched up the dragon just as the man was reaching for his spectacles. He seized the other one and popped them both into the cat basket, which Grandpa was holding out. Several people were now staring at them and muttering. They made for the cliff path, hastily.

At the top Grandpa said grimly, "One more try. Or it's the zoo for the pair of them. We've done our level best."

A breeze had sprung up. Perhaps that helped, or perhaps the dragons had simply got better at flying after a little practice. Anyway, this time they soared upwards and stayed up, floating and flapping over the beach and the people and out over the water. "That's the spirit!" cried Grandpa. Peter clapped and waved.

The dragons whisked their tails and swooped in circles. Their scales caught the sun and glittered until after a few minutes all Peter and Grandpa could see was two twinkling spots of light. And as they watched the two spots plunged down suddenly into the sea, and then sprang up out of it

79

again in a gleaming shower, and then down and up again . . .

"They're fishing!" cried Peter. And he and Grandpa turned away and began to walk slowly back to the road to catch the bus.

Maybe those were the last dragons in Cornwall. Maybe not. There's no telling. As Grandpa said, it's a wonderful thing, Nature.

THE WITCH'S CASTLE

James Reeves

The wood was dark and thick. It was not safe to go there towards nightfall, for evil things happened. In the middle of the wood was an ancient, stern castle, grey and frowning. In it lived a witch, an old woman with hard, wicked eyes, a wrinkled skin, and hands like claws. All who saw her were afraid. Even the animals shrank from her. But few saw her in daylight, for every morning she would turn herself into an owl or a cat – a lean and cruel cat with green eyes and sharp claws. She would roam through the forest catching little creatures to kill and cook for supper in the evening, when she turned herself back into a witch.

The witch had enchanted the ground about her castle, so that if anyone came within a hundred steps of it they were made to stand quite

. still until she gave them leave to move once more. The only creatures she allowed within this magic circle were young girls. If any came into the circle she turned them into birds and fastened them up in cages of basketwork. These she kept in a cold, dark room in the castle, never allowing them to see the light of day. She had more than a thousand of these cages, each with its sad little wood-pigeon, canary or nightingale.

One sunny day in spring two people walked in the forest, not far from the witch's castle. One was a sweet girl named Rosamund, as young and beautiful a maiden as had ever lived in that country. Her friend was a young man called Godfrey. He was tall, straight and handsome. They were happy, for Godfrey had asked Rosamund to marry him, and this she had promised to do if her parents agreed. Neither had any doubt that their parents would be pleased, for hers were fond of Godfrey, and Godfrey's parents loved Rosamund. For hours the two lovers walked in the wood, and forgot about the passing of time. Before long the sun had almost gone down behind the trees.

"We must go home," Godfrey said. "It is late,

and we must not get lost, or we may wander near the witch's castle."

At this Rosamund shuddered, for everyone knew of the witch and her evil ways.

But sad to tell, the two young people lost their path, and as evening fell they sat down for a while under a tree, because Rosamund was weary. Above her in the branches she heard a wood-pigeon crooning sadly to itself.

Rosamund too began to sing softly, and as Godfrey listened, he also became sad. It seemed as if all their happiness was over. All at once he turned and looked through the trees and, as he did so, he became cold with fear. There, for the first time, he noticed the frowning walls of the witch's castle, and knew that danger was near. He was about to seize Rosamund by the hand and escape with her from the danger, when the little song she was singing suddenly turned into the notes of a nightingale. He was too late. Rosamund was not there. Instead, upon a branch of the tree under which she had been singing, sat a little brown bird, and a great screech-owl was circling round it, crying "Tu-whit, tu-whit, tu-whoo!" Rosamund had been changed into a nightingale.

At the same moment Godfrey too fell under the witch's spell. He found himself unable to move. He could not even call out the name of Rosamund.

The screech-owl vanished into the thicket just as the sun faded behind the trees. Almost immediately a hideous old woman appeared and beckoned to the nightingale to come down from its branch. The witch had a basketwork cage in her hand. Into this she put the nightingale, clapping the cage door shut.

The bird was her prisoner. She took it away and placed the cage in the cold, dark room in the castle. Then she returned to where Godfrey stood, still helpless, as if rooted to the place where he had last seen Rosamund.

The witch spoke to him in her cruel, hard voice, telling him he might go on condition that he left the castle as fast as possible and never came near it again.

At last Godfrey found his voice. "Give me back the maiden I love," he begged. "At least let me see Rosamund and speak to her once more."

"You shall never see her again, young man. Now go – and remember, get away from here as far as you can, or you will be turned to stone."

Godfrey had nothing to do but to obey. Stumbling through the darkness, he made off as fast as he could, determined to begin his search for Rosamund on the morrow.

For many days he looked for someone who might help him in his search, but all were terrified at the very thought of the witch and her enchantments. For weeks he strayed here and there, until one night he sank down to sleep at the edge of a meadow, overcome with weariness and despair. His sleep was restless and troubled. Towards morning he had a dream. He dreamed that he saw growing on a hillside a single blood-red flower with a great pearl in its centre. He stooped

and picked the flower and went away with it. Then his dream faded, and he awoke. Somehow he knew that he must find this flower, for it alone could help him to recover the maiden he loved.

So for many days Godfrey went about the countryside, asking everyone he met if they had seen a blood-red flower, growing by itself. No one could help him, and many thought the young man was mad.

Then one day, just as he was beginning to lose hope, the morning sun revealed to him, on a far hillside, something that glowed and sparkled in the grass. He ran towards it, and when he was near enough to see it clearly, he knew that it was what he was looking for – a single blood-red flower with a great drop of dew in the centre, sparkling like a pearl in the sunlight.

The young man picked the flower with trembling hands. Then began the long journey back to the castle. For days he travelled over field and moor, across rivers, through forests, never losing the flower which he believed would bring him happiness.

When he was a hundred steps from the castle, Godfrey was delighted to find that the witch's spells had no power over him. He moved as easily within the magic circle as outside it. He strode up to the great doorway and touched it with the flower. Instantly it flew open. In the courtyard he stood and listened for the singing of birds. He entered an inner door and began to explore the cold and dismal corridors of the castle. At last he heard the sound he had been listening for – the chirping and singing of hundreds of birds. The sound led him to the dark room where the old woman kept her cages. As he entered the room, she was feeding the birds, pushing scraps of crust and seeds between the bars for her hungry prisoners.

At first the witch did not hear Godfrey approach because of the noise of the birds. When she saw him she was seized with anger. She cursed and stormed at the young man, but she had no power over him. She sprang at him with her bony claws, but she could not come within two steps of him. The flower he held had power to break all her enchantments.

The next thing to be done was to find the cage containing his beloved nightingale. He searched high and low, but there were hundreds of nightingales. All at once, Godfrey saw the old woman craftily creeping away with a cage in her hand. Something told him that this must be the cage he had been seeking. Just as the witch reached the door, Godfrey leaped towards her and touched both the old woman and the cage with the scarlet flower. Instantly she lost her power of enchantment. She screamed horribly, and cursed the young man, but he took no notice, and the witch ran from the room and was seen no more.

At the touch of the flower, the basketwork cage had sprung open and the nightingale was free. With a glad burst of song it was turned instantly into the fair maiden whom Godfrey had sought so long. It was his own Rosamund. As she clung to him, her arms fast round his neck, they saw that all the other cages had opened and the birds flown out. They too were turned into young and lovely maidens, so that all the witch's evil was undone.

The young man and his betrothed lost no time in getting as far away from the frowning castle as possible. When they returned home, their parents were overjoyed to see them, and preparations were made for the marriage. Rosamund and Godfrey lived happily for the rest of their long lives, and never feared the enchanted castle again.

THE
WIND CAP

Jane Yolen

There was once a lad who would be a sailor but his mother would not let him go to the sea.

"Tush, lad, what do you know of sailing?" she would say. "You are a farmer's son, and the grandson of a farmer. You know the turn of the seasons and the smell of the soil and the way to gentle a beast. You do not know the sea."

Now the boy, whose name was Jon, had always listened to his mother. Indeed, he knew no one else, for his father had died long ago. If his mother said he did not know the sea, then he believed he did not. So he went about his farm work with a heart that longed for sailing but he did not again mention the sea.

One day as he walked behind the plough, he all but ran over a tiny green turtle on a clod of dirt. He picked the turtle up and set it on his head, where he knew the tiny creature would be safe.

When at last he was done with his ploughing, Jon led the horse to pasture and then plucked the turtle from his head. To his surprise, he found it had turned into a tiny green fairy man that stood upon his palm and bowed.

"I thank you for your kindness," said the manikin.

Jon bowed back but said nothing. For his mother had warned him that, when addressed by the fairies, it is best to be still.

"For saving my life, I will give you your heart's desire," said the green manikin.

Still Jon was silent, but his heart sent out a glory to the sea.

The manikin could read a heart as easily as a page of a book, so he said, "I see you wish to go sailing."

Jon's face answered for him, though his tongue did not.

"Since you put me on your head like a hat to keep me safe, I shall give you a different kind of cap in return, the kind that sailors most desire. A cap full o' wind. But this one warning: Never a human hand will ever be able to take it off."

Then with a wink and a blink, the fairy man was gone, leaving a striped cap behind.

Young Jon clapped the cap on his head and ran home to tell his mother.

When she heard Jon's story, his mother wept and cried and threw her apron up over her head, for a fairy gift is not altogether a blessing.

"No good will come of this wind cap," she said.

But the lad would have none of her cautions. The sailor's cap had bewitched him utterly. The very next day, without even saying farewell to his mother, he ran off to the sea.

Well, the wind cap worked as the fairy had said, and young Jon could summon breezes at will. But still there was that one condition: Never a human hand could take the cap off.

Now, that was bad and that was good. It was bad because Jon could not take his cap off before his captain nor could he take it off for bed. But it was also good. For neither could he lose the cap nor could it be stolen from him.

And since it was wind that sailors called for, and wind that Jon could supply, he soon was a most popular lad, although he had never before been away from shore. For if he twisted the cap to the right, he summoned the east wind. And if he twisted it to the left, he summoned the west. He could turn the cap to call both north and south winds and all the breezes between.

But if that was good, it was also bad. It was good because it made Jon a popular lad. But it was also bad. For once on board ship, he was not again let ashore. The captain would not part with such a prize.

For a year and a day, young Jon did not set foot on land. He saw neither the turn of the seasons nor the turning of the soil. Nothing but the churning of the waves. And there grew in his heart such a yearning to see the land, that it was soon too much for him to bear.

"Oh, let me go ashore just one day," he begged the captain when they had sighted land. "One day, and I swear I will return."

The captain did not answer.

"Just an hour," cried Jon.

But the captain was still.

"Then may you never see land again just as I cannot," shouted Jon.

The captain called his strongest men and they carried Jon belowdecks. And from that time on he was allowed up above neither night nor day, neither near shore nor on the deepest seas.

But Jon could not stop dreaming of the land. He even talked of it in his sleep. As much as he had once longed for sailing, he now longed for farming.

One quiet afternoon, when the sea was as calm and glassy as a mirror and all the sky reflected in its blue, Jon lay fast asleep in his hammock in the hold. And he fell to dreaming again of the land. Only this dream was brighter and clearer than the others, for though he did not know it, the ship stood offshore from his old farm. In Jon's dream the seasons turned rapidly one into the next. And as each turned, so did Jon in his bed, and the cap on his head twisted round and about, round and about, round and about again. It called up a squall from the clear sky that hit the ship without a warning.

The wind whirled about the boat from this side and that, ripping and fretting and gnawing the planks. It tore the sails and snapped the spars like kindling.

"It is *his* fault," the sailors cried, dragging Jon up from below. "He has called this wind upon us." And they fell upon Jon, one and another. They shouted their anger and fear. And they tried to rip the cap from his head.

Well, they could not take it from him, for it was a fairy cap. But they pulled it and twisted it one way and the next, and so the squall became a storm, the mightiest they had ever seen.

The ship's sides gave out a groan that was answered by the wind. And every plank and board shuddered.

Then the captain cried out above his terrified men. "Bring me that cap boy. I shall rid the ship of him." And when Jon was brought before him, the captain grabbed him by the tail of his striped cap and twisted Jon three times and flung him far out to sea.

But the winds called up by the cap spun the ship those same three times around. It turned turtle, its hull to the sky, and sank to the bottom of the sea.

As Jon went under the waves, fingers of foam snatched off the cap. And as it came off, the storm stopped, the sea became calm, and Jon swam ashore. The cap followed in his wake.

When he got to land, Jon picked up the cap and tucked it into his shirt. Then, without a backward glance at the sea, he found his way home to his mother and his farm. He was a farmer's son, no doubt.

But in the winter, when the crops lay gathered in the barn and the snow lay heavy on the fields, he began to dream again of the sea. Of the sea when he had stood his watch and the world rocked endlessly and smelled of salt.

So Jon went to the wardrobe and got out the fairy cap and stood a long moment staring at it.

Then he tucked the cap into his shirt and went out to the field where he had found the fairy man. Looking up the field and down, over the furrows lined with snow, Jon smiled. He placed the wind cap under a stone where he knew the manikin would find it. For magic is magic and not for men. Then he left again for the sea.

And this set the pattern of his days. For the rest of his life Jon spent half the year on a ship and half on the shore, 'til at last he owned his own boat and a hundred-acre farm besides. And he was known far and wide as Captain Turtle, for, as all his neighbours and shipmates knew, he was as much at home on the water as he was on the land.

THE WOODEN CITY

Terry Jones

There was once a poor king. He had a threadbare robe and patches on his throne. The reason he was poor was that he gave away all his money to whomever needed it, for he cared for his people as if each of them was his own child.

One day, however, a wizard came to the city while the King was away. The wizard summoned all the people into the main square, and said to them: "Make me your king, and you shall have all the gold and silver you ever wanted!"

The townsfolk would not agree, however, so the wizard said: "Make me your king or I will turn you all to wood!" But still the townsfolk would not agree. Whereupon the wizard climbed to the top of the tallest tower in the city. He took a live dove and tore out its feathers and dropped them one by one out of the tower, chanting:

Feather touch the earth
And another turns to wood.

Now that poor dove had as many feathers on its back as there were people in that city and, by the time the wizard had finished, everyone in the city had been turned to wood.

When the King arrived back, he found the gates of the city shut and no one to open them. So he sent his servant to find out what was the matter. The servant returned, saying he could not find the gatekeeper, but only a wooden mannequin dressed in the gatekeeper's uniform, standing in his place.

At length, however, the gates were opened, and the King went into the city. But instead of cheering crowds, he found only wooden people, each standing where they had been when the wizard cast his spell. There was a wooden shoemaker sitting working at a pair of new shoes. Outside the inn was a wooden innkeeper, pouring some beer from a jug into the cup of a wooden old man. Wooden women were hanging blankets out of the windows, or walking wooden children down the street. And at the fish shop, a wooden fishmonger stood by a slab of rotten fish. And when the King entered his palace, he even found his own wife and children turned to wood. Filled with despair, he sat down on the floor and wept.

Whereupon the wizard appeared, and said to the King: "What will you give me if I bring your people back to life?"

And the King answered: "Nothing would be too much to ask. I would give you half my kingdom."

So the wizard set to work. He ordered a quantity of the finest wood, and took the most delicate tools, with golden screws and silver pins, and he made a little wooden heart that beat and pumped for everyone in that city. Then he placed one heart inside each of the wooden citizens, and set it working.

One by one, each citizen opened its wooden eyes, and looked stiffly around, while its wooden heart beat: tunca-tunca-tunca. Then each wooden citizen moved a wooden leg and a wooden arm, and then one by one they started to go about their business as before, except stiffly and awkwardly, for they were still made of wood.

Then the wizard appeared before the King and said: "I have come to claim half your kingdom."

"But," cried the King, "my people are still made of wood, you have not *truly* brought them back to life."

"Enough life to work for me!" cried the wicked old wizard. And he ordered the wooden army to throw the King out of the city and bolt the gates.

The King wandered through the world, begging for his food, and seeking someone who could bring his subjects back to life. But he could find no one. In despair, he took work as a shepherd, minding sheep on a hill that overlooked the city, and there he would often stop travellers as they passed to and fro and ask them how it was in the great city.

"It's fine," they would reply, "the citizens make wonderful clocks and magnificent clothes woven out of precious metals, and they sell these things cheaper than anywhere else on earth!"

One night, however, the King determined to see how things were for himself. So he crept down to the walls, and climbed in through a secret window, and went to the main square. There an extraordinary sight met his eyes. Although it was the dead of night, every one of those wooden citizens was working as if it had been broad daylight. None of them spoke a word, however, and the only sound was the tunca-tunca-tunca of their wooden hearts beating in their wooden chests.

The King ran from one to the other saying: "Don't you remember me? I am your King." But they all just stared at him blankly and then hurried on their way.

At length the King saw his own daughter coming down the street carrying a load of firewood for the wizard's fire. He caught hold

of her and lifted her up and said: "Daughter! Don't you remember me? Don't you remember you're a Princess?"

But his daughter looked at him and said: "I remember nothing. I am only made of wood."

So the King leapt on to a box in the main square and

cried out: "You are all under the wizard's spell! Help me seize him and cast him out!"

But they all turned with blank faces, and replied: "We are only made of wood. We can't do anything."

Just then, the wizard himself appeared on the steps of the palace, arrayed in a magnificent robe of gold and silver, and carrying a flaming torch.

"Ah ha!" he cried. "So you thought you'd undo my work, did you? Very well . . ." And he raised his hands to cast a spell upon the King. But before he could utter a single word, the King seized the bundle of firewood that his daughter was carrying and hurled it at the wizard. At once the flame from the wizard's torch caught the wood, and the blazing pieces fell down around him in a circle of fire that swallowed him up. And as the fire raged, the spell began to lift.

The King's daughter and all the others shivered, and the tunca-tunca-tunca of their wooden hearts changed to real heartbeats, and they each turned back into flesh and blood. And when they looked where the wizard had been, there in his place they found a molten heap of twisted gold and silver. This, the King had raised up on a pedestal in the main square, and underneath he had written the words:

"Whoever needs gold or silver may take from here."

But, do you know, not one of those townsfolk ever took a single scrap of it as long as they lived.

I wonder if it's still there?

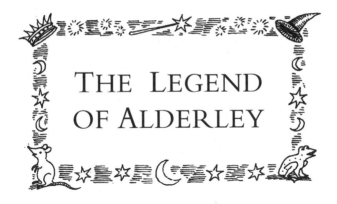

THE LEGEND OF ALDERLEY

Alan Garner

At dawn one still October day in the long ago of the world, across the hill of Alderley, a farmer from Mobberley was riding to Macclesfield fair.

The morning was dull, but mild; light mists bedimmed his way; the woods were hushed; the day promised fine. The farmer was in good spirits, and he let his horse, a milk-white mare, set her own pace, for he wanted her to arrive fresh for the market. A rich man would walk back to Mobberley that night.

So, his mind in the town while he was yet on the hill, the farmer drew near to the place known as Thieves' Hole. And there the horse stood still and would answer to neither spur nor rein. The spur and rein she understood, and her master's stern command, but the eyes that held her were stronger than all of these.

In the middle of the path, where surely there had been no one, was an old man, tall, with long hair and beard. "You go to sell this mare," he said. "I come here to buy. What is your price?"

But the farmer wished to sell only at the market, where he would have the choice of many offers, so he rudely bade the stranger quit the path and let him through, for if he stayed longer he would be late to the fair.

"Then go your way," said the old man. "None will buy. And I shall await you here at sunset."

The next moment he was gone, and the farmer could not tell how or where.

The day was warm, and the tavern cool, and all who saw the mare agreed that she was a splendid animal, the pride of Cheshire, a queen among horses; and everyone said that there was no finer beast in the town that day. But no one offered to buy. A weary, sour-eyed farmer rode up out of Macclesfield as the sky reddened the west.

At Thieves' Hole the mare would not budge: the stranger was there.

Thinking any price now better than none, the farmer agreed to sell. "How much will you give?" he said.

"Enough. Now come with me."

By Seven Firs and Goldenstone they went, to Stormy Point and Saddlebole. And they halted before a great rock imbedded in the hillside. The old man lifted his staff and lightly touched the rock, and it split with the noise of thunder.

At this, the farmer toppled from his plunging horse and, on his knees, begged the other to have mercy on him and let him go his way unharmed. The horse should stay; he did not want her. Only spare his life, that was enough.

The wizard, for such he was, commanded the farmer to rise. "I promise you safe conduct," he said. "Do not be afraid; for living wonders you shall see here."

Beyond the rock stood a pair of iron gates. These the wizard opened, and took the farmer and his horse down a narrow tunnel deep into the hill. A light, subdued but beautiful, marked their way. The passage ended and they stepped into a cave, and there a wondrous sight met the farmer's eyes – a hundred and forty knights in silver armour, and by the side of all but one, a milk-white mare.

"Here they lie in enchanted sleep," said the

wizard, "until a day will come – and come it will – when England shall be in direst peril, and England's mothers weep. Then out from the hill these must ride and, in a battle thrice lost, thrice won, upon the plain, drive the enemy into the sea."

The farmer, dumb with awe, turned with the wizard into a further cavern, and here mounds of gold and silver and precious stones lay strewn along the ground.

"Take what you can carry in payment for the horse."

And when the farmer had crammed his pockets (ample as his lands!), his shirt, and his fists with jewels, the wizard hurried him up the long tunnel and thrust him out of the gates. The farmer stumbled, the thunder rolled, he looked, and there was only the bare rock face above him. He was alone on the hill, near Stormy Point. The broad full moon was up, and it was night.

And although in later years he tried to find the place, neither he nor any after him ever saw the iron gates again. Nell Beck swore she saw them once, but she was said to be mad, and when she died they buried her under a hollow bank near Brindlow wood in the field that bears her name to this day.

THE MAGIC RING

A Persian Folk Tale
Retold by Fiona Waters

Many moons ago in ancient Persia, there was a poor orphan boy called Cassim who lived with his uncle in a tumbledown house in the poorest part of a great city. It was a happy household, for Cassim's uncle had a huge family, but there was very little money to spare. So when he was tall enough to see over the top of the stalls in the bazaar, Cassim decided he must try to earn his own living. His uncle was sad to see him go, but, truth to tell, he was secretly relieved to have one less mouth to feed.

"Cassim, we shall all miss you, but you have a kindly disposition and I am sure you will make your way successfully in this world," said his uncle. "Take this bag, which contains ten pieces of silver, and a special cake that your aunt has baked for you. Go well, Cassim, and our blessings with you," and his uncle enveloped him in a huge hug.

So Cassim left the poor house and made his way towards the city gates. He thought he might be able to find work with one of the mighty camel caravans belonging to the rich merchants that called into the city for fresh supplies as they criss-crossed the desert. In the entrance to a shady courtyard he came across a group of raggedy boys teasing a little white mouse. The poor creature was shivering with fright as she darted hither and thither, trying to avoid the rough feet of the boys.

Cassim bent down and scooped the little creature up in his hands and stroked her gently. The boys rushed up to Cassim and jostled him, demanding the return of the mouse, but Cassim popped her in his pocket and, facing the leader of the gang, said, "You shall not have this poor creature back if all you want to do is torment her. Here, take this silver piece and leave us alone!"

A silver piece was a fortune to the boys, so they were happy to run away to the sweetmeat stall, the mouse quite forgotten. Cassim took the little white mouse out of his pocket and was utterly astonished when she looked at him and said, "Thank you, master. Some day I shall repay you for your kindness and generosity."

A talking mouse! Now that was something special. Cassim smiled as he continued on his way, pausing only to share a piece of his aunt's cake with the mouse. The city was very large and sprawling, and it wasn't until dusk was falling that he finally found himself under the towering city walls. He decided to wait for daylight before venturing out into the desert and so looked for somewhere that he and the white mouse might sleep safely out of harm's way. By good fortune he found a pile of hay by a well in a secluded corner, and he and the white mouse settled down for the night.

The next morning, Cassim was woken by the sound of furious barking and yelping. As he dashed the sleep from his eyes, he saw a cross-looking man dragging a scruffy white dog by a frayed rope towards the well. To his horror, Cassim realized that the man intended to drop the poor dog down the well.

"Stop! Stop! What are you doing with that dog?" demanded Cassim angrily.

"He is worse than useless and I have no need for a dog that is not fierce enough to guard my house," blustered the man, tugging at the frayed rope.

"Here," said Cassim, scrambling to his feet. "Take these three silver pieces. I will look after him."

The man snatched the silver pieces and, flinging the rope in Cassim's direction, rushed off before Cassim could change his mind. The white dog came and sat quietly at Cassim's feet and, looking up at him most earnestly, said, "Thank you, master. Some day I shall repay you for your kindness and generosity."

Well! Now Cassim had a talking mouse *and* a talking dog! Surely fortune was smiling on him. He gave the dog a large slice of his aunt's cake, and he and the mouse shared another piece before they all set off through the mighty wooden gates and out of the city.

The city lay in a green and fertile oasis. Water from the rivers that rose high in the mountains tumbled down and formed deep pools that were fringed by palm trees. But as far as the eye could see there was nothing but undulating sand dunes spreading out from the oasis, shimmering and golden in the early morning light. With the white mouse safely tucked in his pocket, Cassim and the white dog wandered a little way from the city gates. Even at such an early hour the heat was considerable, so Cassim took shelter behind a thick thorn bush and waited to see what he would see.

After a while, the sound of myriad roughcast bells was carried across the sand and soon a great string of camels swayed into view. They were heavily laden with all kinds of bulky bundles, but their bridles were richly inlaid and their saddles were of the finest tooled leather. It was clearly a

115

rich merchant's caravan. Cassim straightened his shoulders, brushed the sand from his baggy trousers and waited until he saw the merchant himself. His saddle was the most splendid, and his flowing robes were of the finest linen. Cassim ran alongside the great loping camel and called up to the merchant.

"O noble master, there are many ways in which a useful boy like myself might prove his worth to you on your long journey. Would you take me on to work as you travel with the caravan?"

The merchant squinted into the sun and then scowled at Cassim (unfortunately Cassim had chosen badly, for the merchant was not a kindly man, as you shall see). He answered roughly, "If you are indeed a useful boy, then get along and present yourself to the caravan master. He will find you plenty to do, but don't expect to be paid much. I haven't money to waste." And he spurred the camel on without a backward glance.

The caravan was stopping to rest, so Cassim hurriedly looked for the caravan master. Though he was just as unfriendly as the merchant, the caravan master grudgingly agreed to take Cassim on for a miserly amount of money and then promptly told him to clean the sand from the feet of every camel. This was a huge and difficult job, as camels are very grumpy beasts and much given to spitting when they are cross. But Cassim was determined to prove his worth, so he set to with a will, leaving the white mouse and the white dog curled up together on his jacket. The caravan master came by every now and again to shout at Cassim to get him to work faster, but otherwise no one spoke to him all day. His throat was parched and his eyes gritty with dust when he finally returned to the white dog and the white mouse. They persuaded the exhausted Cassim to eat the last piece of his aunt's cake before he fell into a deep sleep, the mouse once more in his pocket and the dog at his feet.

Early the next morning, Cassim was woken by a hard kick. There stood the caravan master. "Get on your feet, boy! There is much to do before we set off. We are travelling many miles today," he bellowed. Cassim ran frantically after him as he shouted out more orders. The camels were obstinate and bad-tempered, but soon the great caravan was on its feet and ready to ride.

And this became the pattern of Cassim's days: not enough sleep or food and nothing but harsh treatment from the caravan master. Cassim was brave and he was prepared to work hard, but he began to think this was not the best way for him to make his fortune.

The white dog looked at Cassim and said, "Wherever you go, master, we will go with you."

And the little white mouse added, "Be assured of that, Cassim."

Greatly heartened by their support, Cassim decided that he had nothing to lose. The caravan master was clearly a brute and a cheat who would never pay Cassim what he was owed, and Cassim did not feel it was his destiny to be ill treated by such a man. So when the caravan halted by a deep and shady pool so the camels might drink, Cassim and the white dog and the little white mouse crept away as silently as shadows and hid behind a clump of thorn bushes. Soon the camels lumbered to their feet again, and the caravan slowly wound its way over the sand dunes until the very last camel was out of sight. Cassim breathed a sigh of relief but then looked sorrowfully at his two companions.

"We may well have escaped from the hands of that cruel caravan master, but what will happen to us now? I have but six silver pieces in my pocket, a crust of very dry bread and no water. And no sign of another rich merchant who might have a job for me, and . . ."

But before he could continue in this doleful manner, the little white mouse spoke. "All is not lost, Cassim. Remember why the caravan stopped here in the first place! At the very least we have plenty to drink." And she pointed towards the pool, which did look very inviting. They all looked at each other in delight.

"Of course!" said Cassim, and he scampered down to the pool, the white dog bounding by his side and the little white mouse clasped safely in his hand. But the first thing they saw when they reached the water's edge was a huge and beautiful silver fish, gleaming on the hot sand. It was gasping for breath and flapping frantically in its efforts to reach the water.

Cassim did not hesitate but scooped the fish up, very carefully, so he did not damage any of the glistening scales, and slid it into the water. The fish lay still for a moment then darted away towards the centre of the pool where, with a graceful flick of its tail, it dived deep, deep down into the dark blue water. Cassim peered down at the water for a moment. Then he and the white dog and the little white mouse lay down and drank to their hearts' content.

As Cassim leant back on his heels, his thirst quenched momentarily, there was a glittering flash of silver as the fish suddenly reappeared. It swam right up to the edge of the pool and dropped a finely wrought golden ring on the sand.

"You saved my life, Cassim," it said in a soft fluting voice. "Please accept this magical ring as a sign of my gratitude. Whatever you might need, you only have to rub the ring once and your wish will be granted. You must take very great care of this gift for should anyone else find out its properties, you may be sure they will try to take it from you." And with a swirl of water, the fish vanished before Cassim even had time to say thank you.

"Well!" said the white dog. "Here is a stroke of good fortune. Now we can have something to eat!"

Cassim bent down and picked up the ring.

It glittered in the light and felt very heavy in his hand.

"Rub the ring quickly, master," laughed the white mouse, "for I am starving!"

Cassim was still bemused by the sudden change in his fortunes, so it was a moment or two before he realized just what a treasure lay in his hand. But then he rubbed the ring and in a slightly tremulous voice asked, very politely, if they might have something to eat. There was a crack of starched linen and a gleaming white tablecloth appeared on the sand, very quickly followed by golden plates piled high with all manner of delicious-looking food – saffron rice, gently steaming chicken, fresh green vegetables and glistening candied fruits. A jewelled plate positioned itself very carefully in front of Cassim, followed by a silver bowl for the white dog and a tiny glass saucer for the white mouse. For quite some time all was silent as the three friends ate steadily, for they were all very hungry indeed – but once their initial hunger was eased, they looked at each other with very satisfied smiles.

"Well, master," said the white dog, "that was delicious. But now you need to make sure we have a roof over our heads for the night. Why don't you ask the ring for a magnificent palace?"

Cassim patted the dog fondly. "I don't know about a magnificent palace, but we can certainly ask for a house with rooms for us all and comfortable beds," he said, rubbing the ring once more. Instantly, a particularly inviting bed, scattered with deep pillows covered in silk and a huge billowing quilt, appeared. Without another thought, Cassim sank gratefully into its enveloping comfort, the white dog at his feet and the white mouse curled by the pillows.

When Cassim opened his eyes the following morning, he wondered if he was still dreaming. Servants were bustling about, pulling back heavy damask curtains from gleaming windows, laying out silken trousers and an embroidered waistcoat and a pair of elaborately tasselled slippers, and, most wondrously of all, placing a tray of steaming jasmine tea and freshly baked bread on the table beside the bed.

"Where am I?" asked the bewildered Cassim.

"Why, master, in your own palace," replied a servant, bowing very low.

Cassim rubbed his eyes in growing delight. The magic ring had obviously considered the comfortable bed he had requested should be in equally comfortable surroundings. Once he was dressed, Cassim wandered round the palace, the white dog by his side and the mouse in his pocket. There were endless rooms, all richly furnished and decorated, and wherever he went a great trail of servants followed, ready to cater for his every need. Outside the palace, the splendours continued. Gorgeous gardens bloomed as if by magic (which it most certainly was) out of the desert sands. There were shady avenues of trees, and sparkling fountains, and shady arbours to sit in. Cassim was overwhelmed at the sudden change in his fortunes.

For many long months Cassim and the white dog and the white mouse lived in great harmony and contentment, never going short of a meal and always sleeping in warmth and comfort. The white dog had his own special kennel and an endless supply of tasty bones. The white mouse had her own tiny palace, where everything was mouse-sized, and she too was happy.

Then one day a great caravan with many camels arrived at the palace gates. It was none other than the rich merchant who had treated Cassim so ungenerously. He was greatly astonished to see such a rich palace where previously there had been nothing but endless burning sand, and even more astonished when Cassim greeted him as the owner. Now Cassim had a great deal to learn about the ways of evil men, and in his innocence he did not hesitate to tell the merchant all about how he came by his great fortune, and, more crucially, he told him all about the magic ring.

"I should very much like to look on this marvellous ring," said the merchant slyly.

Cassim held out his right hand where the ring gleamed on his little finger. The merchant leaned

forward as if to look more closely, but, moving as fast as lightning, he wrenched the ring off Cassim's finger and, rubbing it swiftly, he wished for himself and the entire palace to be transported to a far-off island in the middle of a great sea. In a blink of an eye, Cassim and the white dog and the white mouse found themselves by the same pool where they had first met the fish. Cassim sank to his knees in despair. His beautiful palace was a mere dream, and once again he was poor and without a roof over his head.

A wet nose pushed into his hand. "Dear master, do not be sad. Mouse and I are still with you, and we will never forsake you."

Cassim stroked the white dog on his head and lifted up the white mouse with gentle fingers. "Indeed I am blessed with your friendship, but I have let you down badly. How shall we ever get the magic ring back again?" he said sadly.

"By looking, dear master," said the white dog

quietly. "Such a great wonder cannot remain hidden forever. Someone will tell us a strange thing and we will know that the ring is at the heart of the matter. Let us set off in search of our lost palace, and we will see what we shall see."

So the three friends set off on their quest. Long and hard they travelled, but never a mention of the magic ring or the fabulous palace did they hear. They crossed barren wastes and passed through many a lush oasis, over mountains and alongside rolling oceans until they were footsore and weary. But never once did the white dog falter and never once did the white mouse complain.

One day they were sitting below a date palm on the shores of a great blue ocean, eating their meagre supper, when a brightly coloured bird fluttered down to pick up the crumbs that Cassim had scattered. He was only mildly surprised when the bird began talking, for did he not travel with a talking dog and a talking mouse, and had they not met a talking fish?

"Thank you for your kindness," the bird said. "I have travelled far today, over the blue seas and back again. And I saw the most wondrous sight," the bird continued. "Where there had only been a rocky island before, I flew over a fabulous palace, glittering in the sunlight."

The three friends sat up, all tiredness vanished as they plied the bird with questions as to exactly where the island was.

"Without doubt it is *our* palace, master," said the white dog excitedly. "We have found it!"

"Yes, but how shall we reach it?" sighed Cassim. "We have no boat and our bird friend has told us that the island is far over the blue seas."

"This is our chance to repay your kindness, master," said the white dog and the white mouse together.

"I can swim to the island . . ." said the white dog.

". . . while I shall sit on his head," said the brave mouse. "We will return with your ring or else die in the attempt." And without more ado they sprang into the sea and began swimming strongly in the direction the bird had described.

Cassim was greatly distressed. How could two such tiny animals survive such a journey, and what would he do without his friends? He was ready to dive in after them, but the bird laid a soft wing on his arm and said, "Let them try, Cassim. There is magic at work here. I can feel it. Perhaps the ring knows its rightful owner is at hand. Let them try."

All night Cassim paced along the shore, straining his eyes out to sea. Morning dawned, but there was no sign of his plucky friends. He sank to his knees and wept, feeling all was lost. The bird circled round his head, cooing gently to try to soothe him.

Meanwhile, far out to sea, the white dog was still swimming bravely, but he was growing weary and his heart began to fail him. Then the white mouse cried out, "There it is! I can see the island, and oh! how the palace glitters in the first rays of the sun. Have courage, my friend, we are nearly there."

And so, cheered on, the white dog lifted his head once more and swam for all he was worth. The two friends were soon splashing through the shallows, and, with a bursting heart, the dog gave a huge bark of triumph. They had reached the island. As soon as the white dog had recovered from his exertions, they set off towards the palace. Being small, they were able to slip in through the cool corridors, and after some searching they found the rascally merchant, snoring in his bed. The precious ring lay in a jewelled casket on a table close to his hand, and it was guarded by two very fierce-looking black cats with huge green eyes that gleamed in the dim light. The two friends retreated out of the room.

"Now what shall we do?" asked the white mouse.

The two animals sat and thought hard for quite a while. Then the white dog grinned and bent down to whisper in the mouse's ear.

"You must creep very, very quietly round to the back of the bed and tug the merchant's hair as hard as you can manage. If we are lucky, he will think it

is the cats and he will shoo them outside," said the white dog. "Then you can pick up the ring, and we will make our way back to Cassim as fast as ever possible."

So the incredibly brave little mouse slipped quietly back into the room, as quiet as only a mouse can be. She made her way on tiny, silent paws to the back of the bed and tugged the merchant's long hair as hard as she could. Bellowing in pain, he woke up, cursing the cats, who were, of course, the only creatures he thought were in the room. Then, with a heave of the bedclothes, he slumped back down, threatening the cats with all kinds of terrible punishments if they disturbed him again. The cats looked down their noses at him, but their eyes narrowed into slits as they stalked behind the bed. They could smell a mouse, so there must be a mouse. The white mouse trembled with fear, but she was well hidden, and the cats soon got fed up looking and sidled back beside the bed again.

After a few moments, the white mouse again pulled the merchant's hair as hard as she could.

This time, he leapt out of bed and flung the cats out of the room, failing in his rage to see the white dog hidden in the doorway. The merchant stumped back to bed, and soon loud snores told the white mouse that he was fast asleep again. She slipped round the bed, up onto the table, and, snatching up the ring in her paws, ran as fast as she could out of the door and up to where the dog was hiding. The two creatures raced out of the palace as if all the black cats in the world were after them and soon were back down by the water's edge. The little white mouse climbed up onto the white dog's head, the magic ring clasped firmly in both paws,

and the dog began the long swim back to Cassim.

With joy in their hearts, the swim back did not seem so long and soon the three friends were reunited, the brightly coloured bird hopping about the sand in the general excitement. Cassim held the ring in his hands and rubbed it carefully.

"Please bring back our palace, but leave the wicked merchant on the island where he can reflect on his evil ways at his leisure," he cried and in a twinkling there they all were, sitting in a shady arbour by a splashing fountain. It was as if they had never been away. The servants clustered round, bringing all manner of cooling drinks and sweetmeats, and telling Cassim how pleased they were to be serving him once more. It came as no surprise to Cassim to learn that the merchant had been a cruel and demanding master who never said "please" or "thank you" but generally made everyone's life a misery.

Cassim and his faithful friends lived in great contentment for many, many years in their palace, never forgetting how much they owed to each other. And what of the magic ring? Well, I am pleased to say Cassim kept it locked up very safely in the deepest vault and he always wore the key round his neck where no one could possibly steal it from him ever again!

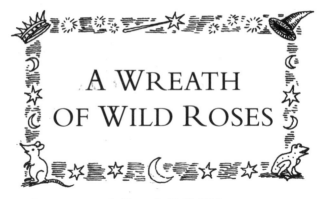

A WREATH OF WILD ROSES

A French Folk Tale
Retold by Barbara Sleigh

Once upon a time, there was a woodcutter, who had two daughters. Both had blue eyes, and rosy cheeks, and golden hair when they were little girls, but as they grew up, Maria became bad-tempered and sour as a green apple, so that her face was covered with crosspatch wrinkles; and because she was too lazy to brush it, her hair looked grey and dusty and hung down like a wet mop. If everyone called her ugly, it was entirely her own fault. But her sister, Mariette, was as pretty as a clean cheerful willing face could make her.

One day, when the woodcutter came home from work, he said, "Bless my buttons if I haven't left my axe behind in the forest. Now I shall have to go all the way back to fetch it, and me with a great blister on my heel!"

"Don't worry, father," said Mariette, "I'll go and

fetch it for you." And she gave him a kiss and set out, while Maria just scowled, and hid herself so that no one should ask her to go too.

Mariette had barely started on her walk when the rain came down like silver needles; so she put her old shawl over her head, and jumped over the puddles as well as she could. By the time she reached the clearing where she knew her father had been working, the rain had stopped and the sun came out. There she saw the axe, fixed in the stump of a tree. On the handle perched two snow-white doves, who were wet and shivering with cold. "Coo-coo-roo!" cooed the doves unhappily. "Coo-coo-roo!"

"You poor little birds!" said Mariette, and she dried their feathers with her shawl, and warmed them between her hands. Then she fed them with the crust she had kept to cheer herself on her long walk home. When they had pecked up every crumb, a little dwarf, dressed all in yellow, stepped from behind a bush, and with a whirr of white wings the doves flew onto his shoulders, cooing excitedly in his pointed ears. "Coo-coo-roo!" they cried. "Coo-coo-roo!"

The little man listened, nodding from time to time, and when they had finished he said to Mariette: "What can I give you as a reward for your kindness to my doves?"

"But I want no reward," she replied.

"May be," said the Yellow Dwarf. "But my doves

and I would like to give you something. What shall it be, my dear?"

Mariette thought the little man looked as poor as she was herself, and could ill afford to give her anything. But as she did not want to hurt his feelings, she looked hurriedly round and said, after a pause, "I should like – a wreath of wild roses!"

With surprising speed, the Yellow Dwarf picked some strands of the wild roses which hung from the branches of a bush, and with strange flickering movements of his hands wove them into a wreath, and held it out to her.

"How beautiful!" said Mariette, holding it up.

"It is no ordinary wreath," said the Dwarf. "Look closely, my dear."

Then Mariette saw that, perched among the flowers, were dozens of tiny blue birds, no bigger than her thimble.

"Sing, little blue birds! Sing!" cried the Dwarf, and the tiny creatures lifted up their golden bills and sang as sweetly as the nightingale when the moon is full.

Mariette laughed with pleasure, and put the wreath on her head. Then she thanked the Yellow Dwarf, put the axe over her shoulder, and went skipping home. And the wreath sang to her all the way, so that it seemed no distance at all.

When at last she reached the woodcutter's hut, and Maria saw the rosy wreath, and heard the sweet singing of the tiny birds, she said, "*I* want a wreath that sings!" And she grabbed the wreath and put it on. But no sooner had she settled it on her tousled hair, than the wild roses began to fade and drop their pink petals, while the little birds turned to buzzing bluebottles.

"It's a *horrid* wreath!" grumbled Maria, pulling it off her head and flinging it on the floor. "I shall go to the forest myself, and I expect the Yellow Dwarf will give me something much more grand." And, after kicking the faded wreath into a corner, off she went. But when Mariette picked up the wreath and put it on again, at once the drooping roses lifted their heads and bloomed, and the bluebottles ceased their buzzing and became little singing blue birds again.

When Maria reached the clearing in the forest, she was even more bad-tempered than usual, for she had borrowed Mariette's Sunday shoes, and they were much too tight. When she saw the white doves perched upon the tree-stump, she cried, "Get away, you stupid creatures! *I* want to sit there!" And she flapped them away and sat down. Then she kicked off her tight shoes, and waggled her ugly great toes, and began to eat a slab of plum-cake she had brought with her.

The doves looked on with their bright eyes, and hopped round expectantly, but instead of crumbs, Maria threw first one shoe and then the other at the poor birds, crying as she did so, "Do you think I have carried a great heavy piece of cake all this way, just to feed a lot of silly birds? Get away, you greedy guzzlers!" And the doves flew sadly away.

"I wish that dwarf would hurry up," went on Maria. "I want my reward."

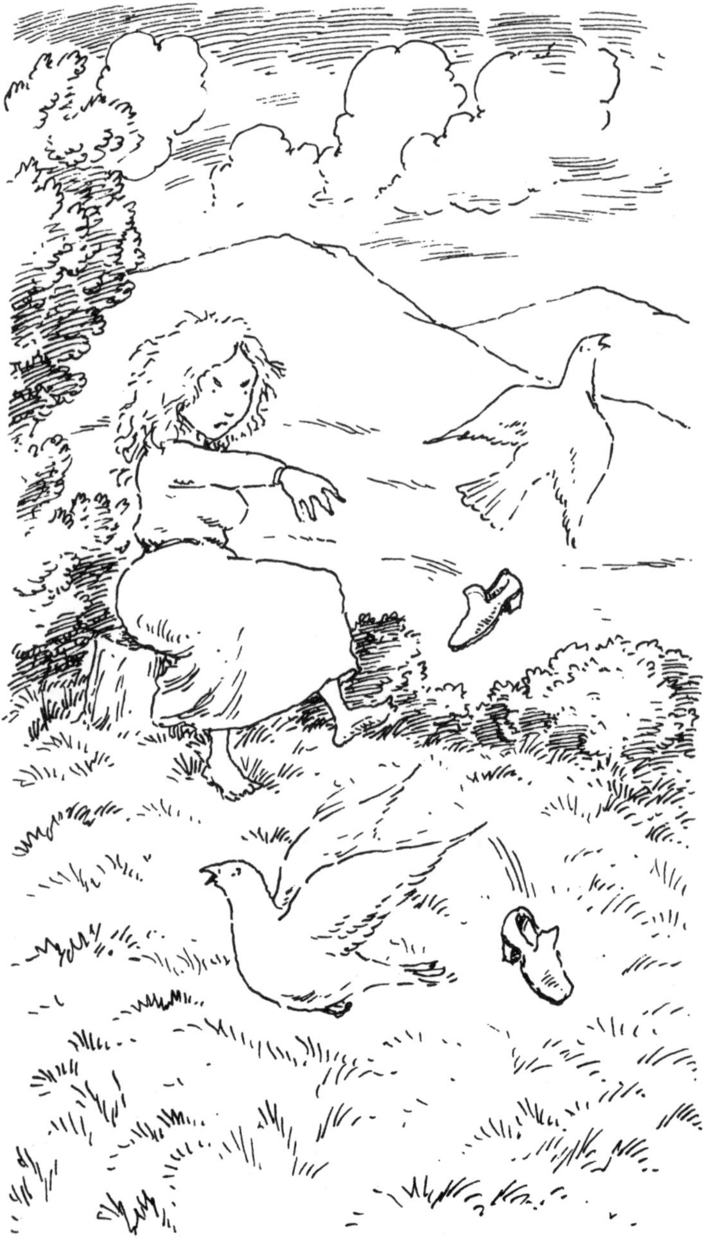

"And you shall have your reward!" said the Yellow Dwarf, stepping suddenly from behind a tree. "I saw it all. 'Greedy guzzlers' you called my doves, so from now on those shall be the only words you can say!"

Maria thought of all kinds of rude things to say to him in reply, but it was no use. The only words that came from her lips were – "Greedy guzzlers!"

When she reached home, she gargled and rubbed her throat till it was sore both inside and out, but it made no difference: she could still only say, "Greedy guzzlers!"

Now the fame of the wreath that sang, and the beauty of the girl who wore it, soon spread abroad, and who should come to see for himself, one day, but the King's son. As soon as he saw Mariette's lovely face, he fell in love with her and asked her to be his wife. They were married in the great cathedral, and all the choir fell silent at the singing of the little blue birds, and the carved saints turned their stone heads to listen.

You would expect me to say that they both lived happily ever after. And so they would have done if it had not been for Maria, who was eaten up with jealousy. Although all she could still *say* was "Greedy guzzlers!" she *thought* to herself, "Why should Mariette live in a King's palace, and wear a golden gown, while I live in a poor hut, in nothing but rags?" And she went on thinking this until a wicked plan came into her head. She had often been told by her father how she and Mariette had once been so alike. Supposing she brushed her hair and tried really hard to look pleasant, could she make herself look as pretty as Mariette? She fetched her sister's hairbrush, and, standing in front of the little cracked mirror, which was all she had, she brushed and brushed until, gradually, the dust of weeks came away, and her hair began to shine almost as brightly as Mariette's had done. Next, she tried looking pleasant. This was a great deal harder. But she smirked and ogled at herself in the mirror until her mouth began to turn up at the corners, and only if you looked closely could you see the crosspatch wrinkles. And at last she really did begin to look like Mariette.

Then she ran as fast as she could to the palace. When she saw Mariette feeding the peacocks on the terrace, the sight of the splendour in which her sister now lived caused Maria to look for a moment as cross as she had ever done, so that Mariette had no difficulty in recognizing her. She was delighted to see her again, and loaded her with presents.

Then she asked her what she would like most to do. Just remembering in time not to speak, Maria made signs that there was nothing she would like better on such a hot day than to bathe. Mariette agreed. And so they made their way to the palace lake, which lay in the middle of a ring of trees. But no sooner had Mariette slipped off her golden gown, than Maria took her by the shoulders and pushed her into the water. Then she picked up the

singing wreath, and threw it after her. And both
Mariette and the wreath sank beneath the still
waters of the lake. Twittering sadly, the blue birds
flew away.

Then Maria crowed with glee, and after
changing her ragged skirt for Mariette's golden
gown, she smoothed her hair and, smirking
cheerfully, made her way to the palace, pushing
rudely past the servants and sometimes, forgetting
that she must hold her tongue, calling the courtiers
"Greedy guzzlers" to their great surprise.

When the Prince found that though his Princess
looked much the same as usual her manners had

become rude and rough, he was sadly troubled. "What is the matter, my dear?" he asked. "And why will you not speak to me? Are you ill?"

But Maria knew better than to try to answer. So the Prince sent for the wisest doctors in the land. But they could find no cure for her silence or her rude, rough behaviour. All she would do was to eat, and throw things at the servants.

Weeks went by, and the Prince grew pale and thin, for he had loved his gentle wife. One day, as he sat silent in his garden, he thought he saw a cloud of tiny blue butterflies, which hovered over the rosebush beneath which he was sitting.

Suddenly, they began to sing — as sweetly as the nightingale when the moon is full. Now butterflies do not sing, so the Prince started up, and recognized at once the little blue birds. "Tell me," he said, "what has happened to the singing wreath? And what can I do to change my Princess back to the gentle wife I loved so well?"

All at once, the blue birds darted off like dragonflies, and the Prince followed. They led him to the lake, where they hovered over the water as though they were waiting for something. As he watched, he saw the water stir and dimple, and, through a ring of shining ripples, rose the real Princess, with the wreath upon her head.

"Dear husband!" cried Mariette. "My jealous sister pushed me into the lake and threw the wreath after me. She did not know that as long as I wear it I can live an enchanted life beneath the water."

"She looks like you, and wears your clothes, but there the likeness ends," said the Prince. "Dear wife, what can I do to break this watery spell and bring you back again?"

"Listen well, my dear," replied Mariette. "For I must return to the mud and ooze at the bottom of the lake. When I sink once more beneath the water, you will find the singing wreath floating on the surface. Take it quickly to the palace, and put it on the head of my cruel sister, and you will see her as she really is."

"What then?" asked the Prince.

"If you wish to save me," said Mariette, "before the sun sets, you must dive to the bottom of the lake. There, in the mud, you will see a hideous great slug. Take it in your arms and carry it to the shore. Remember, whatever it may turn into, hold it fast, or you will never see me again. Above all, make haste. Once the sun has set I can live no longer under the water without the singing wreath."

As she spoke, Mariette sank once more into the lake. Only the ripples showed where she had been. And there, on the surface, floated the singing wreath. It drifted to the bank where the Prince stood. He took it up, and the tiny blue birds settled among the roses, singing joyfully. Then he hurried to the palace, and who should come to meet him but Maria, elbowing her way through the courtiers.

Before she could prevent him, he put the wreath on her head. At once, the roses began to droop, and when Maria saw their fading petals falling to the ground, and heard the singing of the blue birds turn to the buzzing of angry bluebottles, she was so furious that her mouth turned down at the corners, and all the crosspatch wrinkles creased her face again so that she looked as ugly as she had ever done. By the Prince's horrified face she realized that she had been discovered, and, flinging the wreath on the floor, she turned and fled for her life, and was never seen again.

Then the Prince saw that the rim of the sun was just beginning to sink behind a bank of purple cloud, and he ran to the lake as fast as he could go. By the time he came to the wood, a quarter of the sun had sunk behind the cloud. When he reached the lake and dived into the water, only half the crimson circle could be seen.

Down, down he went, to the bottom of the lake, and there, as Mariette had said, he found a hideous great slug. Steeling himself to touch the horrible slimy thing, he shut his eyes and, clasping it in his arms, fought his way up again. Suddenly, he found he was holding not a slug, but a serpent, whose coils twisted themselves round him in such a grip that he could scarcely move.

But he held it fast. Just as he reached the surface the serpent changed into a great bird, whose wings were made of iron and whose beak was of steel, with which it attacked the Prince. But still he held fast, and as he stumbled ashore, the spell was broken, the bird was gone, and in its place was his own dear wife, Mariette. And at that very minute the last of the sun disappeared behind the purple cloud.

Then Mariette and the Prince walked back to the palace hand in hand, in great joy and contentment.

And, this time, they really *did* live happily ever after.

LA CORONA
AND THE
TIN FROG

Russell Hoban

L a Corona was the name of the beautiful lady in
the picture on the inside of the cigar box lid.
She wore a scarlet robe and a golden crown.
Beyond her was a calm blue bay on which a
paddle-wheel steamer floated. A locomotive trailed
a faint plume of smoke across the pink and distant
plain past shadowy palms and pyramids. Far off in
the printed sky sailed a balloon.

But the lady never looked at any of those things.
She sat among wheels and anvils, sheaves of wheat,
hammers, toppled pedestals and garden urns, and
she pointed to a globe that stood beside her while
she looked steadfastly out past the left-hand side of
the picture.

Inside the cigar box lived a tin frog, a seashell, a
yellow cloth tape measure, and a magnifying glass.
The tin frog was bright green and yellow, with

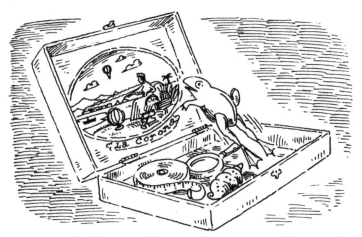

two perfectly round eyes that were yellow-and-black bull's-eyes. He had cost five shillings when new and hopped when wound up. He had fallen in love with La Corona, and he was wound up all the time because of it. He kept trying to hop into the picture with her, but he only bumped his nose against it and fell back into the box.

"I love you," he told her. But she said nothing, didn't even look at him.

"For heaven's sake!" said the tin frog. "Look at me, won't you! What do you expect to see out there beyond the left-hand side of the picture?"

"Perhaps a handsome prince," said La Corona.

"Maybe I'm a handsome prince," said the tin frog. "You know, an enchanted one."

"Not likely," said La Corona. "You're not even a very handsome frog."

"How do you know if you won't look?" said the tin frog. Again he tried to hop into the picture, and again he only bumped his nose and fell back. "O misery!" he said. "O desperation!"

"Pay close attention," said the magnifying glass.

"To what?" said the tin frog.

"Everything," said the magnifying glass. He leaned up against the picture, and the tin frog looked through him. When he looked very close he saw that the picture was made of coloured printed dots. Looking even closer he saw spaces between the dots.

"One doesn't always jump into a picture from the front," said the magnifying glass.

"Do it by the inch," said the tape measure.

"Be deep," said the seashell.

The tin frog thought long and hard. He waited for the moment just between midnight and twelve strokes of the clock. Everything was dark.

The tin frog dropped the seashell over the side of the cigar box. He heard a splash. "Very good," he said. He unrolled the tape measure over the side of the cigar box. Then he hopped,  and found himself in the ocean.

Down, down, down he followed the yellow tape measure in the green and glimmering midnight water. Through coral and sea fans and waving green seaweed he swam, past sunken wrecks and treasures and gliding monsters of the deep, until the tape measure curved up again. Up and up went the tin frog, toward the light, and he came out between the coloured dots of the calm blue bay where the paddle-wheel steamer floated. The dots closed up behind him, and he was in the picture with La Corona.

"Here I am," said the tin frog when he had swum ashore. "I love you."

La Corona

"You look quite different," said La Corona. "You may not be an enchanted prince, but you *are* an enchanting frog."

They were married soon after that. They took a sea voyage in the paddle-wheel steamer. They drifted far and high across the blue sky in the wicker basket of the balloon. And often they travelled past shadowy palms and pyramids in the train pulled by the locomotive that trailed its faint plume of smoke across the pink and distant plain.

When next the cigar box was opened it was empty. In the picture on the lid La Corona and the tin frog smiled at each other. And among the wheels and anvils, sheaves of wheat and hammers were the magnifying glass, the tape measure, and the seashell.

Acknowledgements

The publisher would like to thank the copyright holders for permission to reproduce the following copyright material:

Margaret Baker: "Cinderella's Sisters" by Margaret Baker, from *Tell Them Again Tales* published by Hodder. Reprinted by permission of Hodder & Stoughton Limited. **Winifred Finlay**: "Tamlane" by Winifred Finlay, from *Tales from the Moor and Mountain*. Copyright © 1969 Winifred Finlay. Published in the UK by Egmont Books Limited, London and used with permission. **Vivian French**: "Under the Moon" by Vivian French, from *Singing to the Sun*. Copyright © 2001 Vivian French. Reproduced by permission of Walker Books Ltd., London SE11 5HJ. **Alan Garner**: Extract from *The Weirdstone of Brisingamen* by Alan Garner, published by HarperCollins Publishers. Copyright © Alan Garner 1960. Reprinted by permission of Sheil Land Associates Limited on behalf of the author. **Russell Hoban**: *La Corona and the Tin Frog* by Russell Hoban, published by Cape. Reprinted by permission of David Higham Associates Limited on behalf of the author. **Terry Jones**: "The Wooden City" by Terry Jones, from *Terry Jones Fairy Tales* published by Pavilion Books. Reprinted with permission of Chrysalis Books. **Penelope Lively**: *Dragon Trouble* by Penelope Lively, published by Egmont. Reprinted by permission of David Higham Associates Limited on behalf of the author. **Margaret Mahy**: the author for "The Little World, the Little Sun and the Wonderful Child" by Margaret Mahy. Copyright © Margaret Mahy 2003. **James Reeves**: "The Witch's Castle" by James Reeves, from *The Secret Shoemakers*. Copyright © James Reeves 1966. Reprinted by permission of Laura Cecil Literary Agency on behalf of the James Reeves Estate. **Barbara Sleigh**: "A Wreath of Wild Roses" by Barbara Sleigh, from *Winged Magic*, published by Hodder & Stoughton Children's Books. Copyright © Barbara Sleigh 1979. Reproduced by permission of The Agency (London) Limited, 24 Pottery Lane, London, W11 4LZ fax: 020 7727 9037. All rights reserved. **Fiona Waters**: the author for "The Magic Gifts" and "The Magic Ring" by Fiona Waters. Copyright © Fiona Waters 2003. **Jane Yolen**: "The Wind Cap" by Jane Yolen, from *Parabola Magazine*. Copyright © 1976 Jane Yolen. First appeared in Parabola Magazine, published by The Society for the Study of Myth and Tradition. Reprinted by permission of Curtis Brown Ltd., New York.